WINTER HEART

WINTER HEART

a novel by

B.G. BRADLEY

Benegamah
Press

Hulbert Lake, MI
Canby,OR

Benegamah Press
Hulbert Lake, Michigan
Canby, Oregon

Cover photo by B.G. Bradley
Cover and book design by Matt Dryer

Special thanks to Beth Bennett, Monica Nordeen, & Shantel LaRocque

Printed in the United States of America

For Debbie Taggart, the love of my life.

FOREWORD
By Matt Dryer

The Upper Peninsula of Michigan will always be my home. I've lived in Oregon for the second half of my life, and still do. It is an absolutely beautiful place, but when I say home, I'm almost always referring to the U.P. It was a marvelous place to grow up and leaving was the hardest thing I've ever done.

For as far back as I can remember, I've always wanted to work in the comic book industry. It's a funny thing knowing what you want to do with your life. It turns out it's a pretty rare gift and it was a while before I figured out that most people don't actually know what they want to be when they grow up. Not really. So it stands to reason that people who do know what they want would naturally be drawn to one another. There's a certain understanding. It's kind of like having a secret handshake. They get it. They get you.

Another rare gift is having someone who gets you as teacher. That's where B.G. Bradley comes in. At the time he was my high school English teacher and he was one of those people. He got it. Having someone like that in your corner during your formative years is like skipping a grade.

I didn't know it at the time, but the reason he got me (and that I got him) was because he was a writer. You don't realize a lot of things when you're sixteen years old, and I think I just assumed the teachers powered down for the night after we left and plugged into a wall socket somewhere to recharge. It didn't occur to me at the time that teachers might have other pursuits. Mr. Bradley is a writer. It didn't take long for us to bond. We shared a passion for good storytelling and truth.

After all, what are good stories but the discovery and reflection of truth? Beeg—even now, it's still a little weird to call him Beeg rather than Mr. Bradley—and I continued to debate truths and artistic merit well after I graduated and went off to college. Coming home for holidays and breaks, I would always try to make time to catch up with him and his family. Some of my favorite memories are sitting around the Bradleys' wood stove on a cold winter's night, with a mug of something warm (or a bottle of something cold and sudsy!) discussing life, the universe, and everything.

When career opportunities presented themselves on the West Coast, I took my big leap and left home for good. And as my new life took shape, trips home became shorter and less frequent, and the visits to the Bradley house got fewer and farther between. We managed to catch up every now and again, but the distance made it easier to lose touch. However, the lessons, guidance, and support I enjoyed from our friendship stayed with me . . . and the passion for good storytelling and truth did too.

In 2016, I learned that Beeg was retiring from teaching. It also happens that I was getting married. So that summer my new wife and I came back home and had a reception to celebrate with my Michigan family. To my delight, Beeg and his wife Debbie were able to join us. We picked up, as you do with those kinds of relationships, right where we left off.

In reconnecting with him, he told me about a number of projects he was working on. He was writing a lot and some of the stories he thought I'd enjoy. Naturally, given my background, he told to me about some science-fiction stories he'd been working on. He also mentioned another piece he'd been working on, something very personal . . . a novel. At the time, he seemed to almost be downplaying it, but I told him I'd like to read them all.

Later that fall he emailed me the manuscripts. The autumn and winter seasons are when I long for Michigan the most, so I reached for the one called *Winter Heart*, first.

Within the first few paragraphs I was home … back in the U.P., listening to the snow-muffled footfalls, as the character Ben O'Brien tromped through the woods with his labradors and tested the frozen lake. I could see his breath hang in the cold dry air, and I could see that haunting gray Michigan sky in the dead of winter. So crisp. So cold. So perfect. He had captured it all and transported me there within moments.

What followed was an epic all-night read as his prose and verse washed over me. The sights, sounds, smells, and people of this great land were brought to life right there in my Oregon home. The thing that struck me most, however, was how very personal this story was. It was so honest and sincere. I got to know Beeg in a way I never had before.

When I finished we corresponded at length about it. At first about the story itself, but soon it became about getting it out there into the world. Beeg had been shopping the book to a few bigger publishers, but he wasn't really getting any takers. I wasn't surprised and I told him he could have written *The Grapes of Wrath*, but cold submitting it to a New York publisher is not unlike casting a message in a bottle off into the ocean and hoping someone finds it.

When I first suggested self-publishing, I could tell he was hesitant, but doing it yourself is very much an Upper Peninsula mentality. I also pointed out that "do it yourself" doesn't mean all by yourself. "You handle the writing and the publicity," I said, "and I'll take care of printing and production."

From there, Benegamah Press was formed. You now hold in your hands it's first offering, *Winter Heart*. I hope you find it as compelling, funny, tragic, beautiful, and sincere as I do.

This book speaks truth. The town of Hunter is a fictional place, and yet it is real. The characters are all made up, and yet if you've ever been to Michigan's Upper Peninsula, chances are, you've met every one of them. In some books, the setting of a story is little more than a backdrop. In others, it is as important as any character or plot point. In the case of *Winter Heart*, the setting is everything. Beeg encapsulates the Upper Peninsula experience perfectly. *Winter Heart* strikes a perfect balance of prose and verse, which captures the essence of life in the U.P. and what it truly means to be of a place. This story brings me home.

-Matt Dryer
Canby, Oregon
2017

But all shall be well, and all manner of things shall be well.
-Julian of Norwich

From the Darkness
by Ben O'Brian

In the night, under a full moon
Casting veiled light, throughout the house,
I descend creaking stairs to find my red hunting dog
Sitting tall on the carpet, watching the silver circle.

I make a sandwich, watch catsup drip
onto the pages of *The Dubliners,*
follow its source, see my father's hand,
coated in dark red ooze, clutching
a smallmouth bass just below the gills.

In the night, at the cabin, lying on the bottom bunk,
Blind in the ebony of wilderness,
I hear a loon wail, a coyote howl.

I swim out eight hundred yards from the cabins,
And listen to the conversations traveling
like a single blast of buckshot over the water.

In the night, at home, I hear a noise
like a single strike on a hide drum.
I walk into my children's rooms to see them sleeping,
blanketless and curled.
Their small mouths breathing.

Reeling from regrets of an argument I started,
I walk away form the house,
down the tracks to the path by the pond,
onto the narrow layer of pavement
beneath the brooding rock bluff.
My footfalls turn silent in the moonlight.

In the night, crossing the lake in sharp cold,
I huddle in the stern under camouflage coats.
Look towards the bow where the red dog scents the
wind.
Look with my brother towards the east's growing light.
We are seeking silhouettes with whistling wings.
We are hungry for explosions in the dark.

In the night, on the beach
I sit by the fire with my son.
Speak of a ghost who walks the southeastern shore,
a ghost who may be my father.
I look back up at the cabin
where my wife sits under the one electric lamp,
watches the last of the night,
rocks our youngest slowly in her arms
and listens for sounds from the darkness.

Chapter I
Wolf and Family

February 1, 2016

There's a wolf down in Mud Lake. I feel better saying that. I feel better knowing that. I feel good that I knew exactly what he was, as I stood there by the open water of the channel on the frozen shore next to the beaver dam. Everybody in my family reveres this place. "Here is your water and your watering place," wrote Frost, and I think this is ours. Lots of things happen here. My old dogs' ashes are scattered here. Mine will be too, to a background of Kate and Mike singing to Beethoven's 9th. We have all played here as kids. We have stopped here to think as adults, far from all that "busy monster manunkind" stuff. Anyway, the dogs knew he was a wolf too. Huck, my old chocolate lab, raised his head and smelled him. He couldn't see him if he was three feet away, but that old dog knew him. Tom, the younger chocolate just looked or smelled where Huck's nose was pointing. He saw I think and definitely scented. And the wolf looked or scented at us. They're big, so damned big. This one mostly gray with a big rough, some brown along his flanks. The hair standing on his shoulders was in silhouette against the ice in the morning daylight. He was backlit, is how they would say it in Hollywood I guess. His shoulders seemed to be festooned with feathers with that rough standing out. How strange, somewhat disconcerting, to be looked at by a predator, even from that distance. He just wondered,that wolf. I suppose wolves have been having the same wonder for a long, long time. Just wondered; then he went on his way. I've never been in a wolf's head, but it seems to me I may share his wonder at human beings. People are hard to know, even the people at the bakery in Hunter, even my family living and dead. Maybe especially them.

Cold out. Low teens and dropping fast. I've managed to keep the furnace on and the water going in the camp. I'll build a fire later. Just to clarify, "camp" is what we call our cottages or lake houses here in the U.P., Upper Peninsula of Michigan. So, I'm not sleeping out in the woods in February. Although I have a time or two. Sometimes even as a form of recreation.

There's nobody here but the dogs and me under the gray heavy lid of the sky today. I'm a little lonely if I'm honest with myself. Sometimes I go into a panic, like a small child, with the idea of Gracie gone, Kate off in her own world, Mike…who knows where? I even miss Jen in those moments. Sometimes, when it gets really bad, I even think about my always distant brother Jake.

Absolute spasms of loneliness, hopelessness envelope me then. Then, if I go to the channel, or lose myself in the canyons of some wonderful book, pulled down from the ancient shelves in the camp, or head off on that day trip known as writing a poem, I'm okay. When I'm like this, I sometimes giggle too, unexpectedly. I shock myself sometimes with the sound of it. I wonder who the hell is laughing. I don't judge it, though, when I figure out who just giggled. When I'm at my best I don't judge at all. Judgement of myself and others seems to be receding, but it's a bitter old friend who just won't go out the door. Anyway, like Hemingway pointed out, when you're alone if you seem crazy, but you know you're not crazy, it really doesn't matter.

If I piss in my camp's front yard in the snow, I feel good. Why should that be? There's no "should" I guess, it just is. That makes me laugh. Piss in the snow is funny. Piss is funny. It's onomatopoeia. And the steam rising up and the color is beautiful. We're not supposed to think so. We're not supposed to think that the golden, really golden stream of piss is beautiful. Why? There was a Python routine about bat piss involving George Bernard Shaw and Oscar Wilde… Jesus,

I'm so scattered.

Jesus.

Christ. I like that better. "Christ" sounds not quite so fundamentalist. It doesn't sound as batshit as "Thank you Jaysuz!" I suppose you could say, "Keerist!" and fire off your shotgun. The Christ. It could be a person or a thing, or an idea. Well…it is a noun after all. It could be a new brand of cracker. "Christ crackers, good for your soul!" Spiritual and sacrilegious are not supposed to be the same, but sometimes they are. I think about that when I consider the first miracle of Jesus at the wedding feast. It's a sacrilegious story really, and it's funny. Everybody's getting drunk, Mary, a true Jewish or Catholic mother, tells Jesus they're almost out of wine and why doesn't he use his big deal powers to do something about it. Jesus says, "Quit nagging me, ma!" Then has the servants bring over water casks and transforms the contents. When the head waiter tastes the new wine he balls out the host for saving the good stuff for when everybody's drunk and can't appreciate it. This miracle is about being one of the guys! It's about drinking with your friends, about using whatever powers you have to help out even in fairly mundane situations. We're all in this together. Somebody should tell the supposedly Christian temperance folks and not so subtle racists this.

Religions hold close with buildings. With buildings comes structure. Something that is; something that is not. Something that must not be, should not be. Something that shall be one day. Something that must not be allowed to continue. Restrictions. Prejudices. If you're going to define what you believe within a building with people around you, you also have to define what you don't believe. There's the problem. There's the shit. Maybe, belief is the problem. Maybe we should simply be, in what is, both physically and spiritually. I want to be "catholic" like Thomas Merton not "Catholic", like Pope Benedict. Like Thomas Merton who was a Roman Catholic and a catholic like Gandhi. That is, somebody who believes that there is only one church, the church of humanity and if we can all just quit picking on each other for half a second we can practice our one religion: love, or "charity" as the King

James puts it so eloquently. Until fairly recently, it was okay in the church to be like Merton. Then it wasn't when the neo-Nazis took over. Now after all the scandals and those poor kids, we finally have a truly good man as Pope.

Francis says in a veiled way, "Hey, do what you think is right." He is much like Mother Theresa: Do the work; do the work that needs to be done, whatever you call it.

So I walk and think, like Merton, or Gandhi. Wow, pretty big ego there. Let's just say the three of us all share the commonality of walking and thinking. And I do my very humble work hoping it's for the greater good, not completely unlike Mother T or Pope Francis. Thoreau said all walks are holy. I agree. I want to be a saunterer, a walker to the holy land, as Thoreau put it. I've been walking almost every day since Dad died when I was 14. It has always helped purge the demons for me, beginning with that guilt, about wishing my father was dead, out of pain, over with cancer. It was a very humane thought in retrospect, but a Catholic conscience will never let you get away with that. Dad used to hate to walk. Mom made him to lose weight. He never did lose it until cancer got him. And then the three of us went for forced marches in the snow when he got sick. He hated it even more then, but I know Mom was doing what she thought was best. She always did that. Always said, even when she was dying of cancer at 88 after a long and very meaningful life, "There has to be a course of action." In the end, because of this conviction, she underwent major surgeries which we all thought were fruitless. In that, and perhaps in our winter marches with Dad, she was wrong, but her intent was for the best. When the walks were still just to lose weight, Dad was always sneaking food from the kitchen at the old hospital annex where his dentist's office was. Those kitchen ladies loved him. He was a charmer, with those brown eyes, always with the jokes.

Cancer isn't funny. Cancer is such a hardass. Such a lawyer of the laws of Nature. So unreasonable. So beyond reason, good, evil. Man says "To be; or not to be" cancer says, "I don't give a shit. Just doing my job. Die now and let me be on my way."

That sounds like the younger me. So bitter. So angry. I

still can't be objective about cancer. It was so personal. I was 14 and he was dying, turning into a creature I couldn't fathom. He couldn't help me with my baseball swing. Couldn't help me learn to hunt. Poor Dad. To be denied that, both the joy and frustration of just raising his children is just one of the many ways in which the cosmos seems unfair. He was a better Dad than I am. Maybe because he wasn't so involved. So worried about every moment. The best picture of him we have shows him in the duck blind. He's nearly invisible with his hood up, a smile that's not quite a smile on his face making it somehow more real, more filled with joy. He just liked to be that guy. I get that. I wish I could have told him that I got him.

My son Mike, he'll always be Mike to me, no matter how he insists on Michael, is off somewhere. I don't even know quite where just now. Brazil? Belgium? Running. Running, hiking, skiing, and writing. What the fuck is that? What the fuck is this? My resentment. So stupid. I'm just pissed because he's making his living writing in a way I don't understand. It's not enough for me that he's even in the same profession I am, he has to be doing it exactly as I did or he's not succeeding. Damn it, he's a good son. He's making his way... He's a weird kid. Always was. So open. Then, at some juncture that seems silly to me, filling out a form, trying to explain his feelings, finishing a project, he just crashes, just crashes down into little bits of glass that can't be put back together, that maybe never fit together to begin with. But each one so beautiful...I remember sitting with him at a production of *Richard III,* brilliant production, The Stratford Shakespeare Festival in Canada. It was intermission and he looked up at the twisted trees on the set and said, "The trees are twisted just like Richard: inside and out." I remember my jaw dropped. He was all of ten. First of all, who brings their kid to Richard at 10? but it was okay and I knew it would be because he was Mike. He's a little light that comes on half way through your dream as he came on the scene 32 years into my life. This little dream light, like Mike, is amazing and inexplicable, but somehow you know it anyway. It's familiar, and yet odd. That's him. That's him now. I just want to stop and look...ha...

reflect. Like my beautiful colored glass son.

My tough-as-nails, lovely as daybreak, daughter, Kate. She doesn't need me at all. Glad to have her near, teaching her classes, telling student stories now that I'm all done with that. I like to watch her grade papers. She hates that. Never could let me watch her do anything. Her husband, Dave Loonsfoot, isn't up to her. Intellectually, I mean. She's so smart. He's a good guy though, so who the hell am I to judge? I should listen to Francis. Who could be up to her really?

She can't have kids. She found that out about a year ago. It's got to break her up some ways. Doesn't show; only once in a while around the eyes. Just a twinge, just a hint when she talks about it, which is seldom. "I've got classrooms full of kids," she says. So goddamned tough. I just want to stretch out to her and wrap my arms around her sometimes, anything to just make her let her guard down. Make her cry. But that is just not her way. She's way tougher than I'll ever be. She's like her grandma and like my Grace, who was such a good Mom to them. So willing to let things play out. So unlike me. The beast got her too. Cancer. Shit. Too soon. Too soon, even 15 years later. It may always be too soon to look it right in the face. At least for me. It's better than it was though.

Christ. Hurts my stomach to go to church. Here by this fire is holier, except for when the church is empty or nearly empty. That's how religions should work. The community should come together and build something beautiful and then make a rule, when it's done, that no more than five people can be inside at any one time and all of them must make a permanent vow of silence while they are there. Then once a year…okay…five times, the whole community can come in. They have to come in singing and sing the whole time; never talk. And the same songs will be sung each year…which ones? The one that goes to Beethoven's Ninth whatever that is… "*Joyful, Joyful*"? never can remember…Sibelius's hymn, national anthem of Finland, with the English lyrics about tolerance…*Birmingham Jail, Star of the County Down, Amazing Grace, Jesus Christ is Risen Today, Morning has Broken, Silent Night, The First Time Ever I Saw Her Face.* That's enough. Just shut up and sing. I'd like to tell so many supposed Christians that. They sound so much smarter when they sing, so much more civilized.

They're trying to take away my church. My family's church. They've already taken it from my kids who won't come within a mile of it. Hypocrisy they tell me…well duh…Still, I can't blame them. Mom used to sit on the Parish Council, tough old broad following her course of action. Dad used to count the pews, then tell me the totals, the scamp (He always told me a different number then smirked). Me…I'd rather look at this fire. It talks. It talks and says amazing things which I never quite hear and not just because I'm going deaf. We're all deaf. Living and dying is just a way of sorting out what to listen to. It's all the noise. That's why we can't hear. It's the opposite of deafness really. We hear too much and most of it is shit. The music of the spheres is completely drowned out most of the time. That's why I come here. The only time church is close to this is just before the Easter Vigil when there's a fire out front and all those candles later inside, everyone holding one. And then when there's singing, even bad singing and nobody talking. Nobody filling up the air with their stupid opinions. Especially me.

I don't go out at night here enough. Out under the stars. I seem to just look out the porch window. It couldn't be prettier. The clear sky. The Milky Way above the ice. So why don't I go out? Something inexplicable, which maybe will come to me in a dream months from now. Then I'll go out under the stars at night. It's funny I always think its weird that the stars are over the trees. My brain is broken that way. I can't think of the stars as Nature. They seem like science. Too much Arthur C. Clarke as a kid I think. I got to thinking that the stars were about science and the trees were about Nature. I wasn't making it all one thing. Should have read more Thoreau in junior high before the sci fi got entrenched. So why won't I go out at night? The cold? Am I scared? Maybe a little, yeah. I can't say of what. I've seen bears often, and the wolves around here a time or two like today. When I see them they don't seem frightening. Still, they remain so in my imagination. Old cave men die hard.

Stars lighting the snow
Make a bleeding hand up to the sky
Blood up from the frozen water and land
Light and blood co-mingle
Which is the source?

Grace never loved this lake in ice. She liked the colors, but said it made her too sad to see it white. Like Kate and Mom, she never liked to be sad. She thought it was a waste of time I think. Or was it that she just couldn't bear it. Was she afraid that if she started crying she'd never stop. Was and is that the way with all three of these fine women? I just don't know them that well. At the end Grace was white. So white. She blended with the damned hospital sheets when they weren't stained red. Maybe one reason I come here when it's cold is that I don't miss her here now. She never came to see the sheet ice form, to see it solid as any road. Summer was her time here. She would have loved seeing the water running northwest through the channel though. Down where the dogs and I saw the wolf today. Our channel. It has to get awfully cold to make the water stop running. It was lively down there today. The beaver and otter use it. It's hope running in that open water really. It can get grim, but hope runs under that ice. She would have liked that, but maybe it's better that there are no memories of her here in this cold season

I hear it
Hear the water—
Sunlight eggs it on
This little channel defying the cold
Makes me bold and young
I open my eyes and see it sizzle by
and my bones hurt in the wind
I want to run with this young water
Run small water wild
Oblivious to doom

Hope builds in that little stream. The Earth dreams of summer. Summer is just as real as an idea: the Earth's idea under snow. It's almost better there before it has had a chance to sprout and grow and grow older and decay and die. That's morbid, but it's true. Life heads towards death always, but death heads towards life. Merton is always talking about our purpose on earth simply being preparation for death. Maybe death then is just preparation for rebirth. Or is it all more instantaneous than that. If I can just stay in this moment, with the wolf eyeing the pups and me. See all that there is in that one short series of seconds. Suck all the marrow out of life. It's so simple if that's it. Ha. There's really no doubt that's it.

Grace 15 years gone, Dad 40, and Mom, that tough old bird at 88 just eight years ago. On her death bed she was giving instructions, and I told Jake, Jen, and I had it handled. "You never stop being a parent." She said. Not "a mom", "a parent". "Mom" is too sentimental a word for her, always the old teacher. She was fearsome. Terrified those ninth graders. Conjugated their souls and diagramed their future plans for them. And they loved her, even her hospice nurse Carrie, whom she had saved from a young pregnant girl life simply by telling her, "You're not dropping out. Get back in here!" She was something, a pistol, a pill, a piece of work. Sometimes as a professor I had some of that, but I was more the flight of fancy school. I never had to be tough because I looked it. Kate always calls me on it. She got a double dose from Mom and Grace. Ol' Gracie was never a touchy feely psychiatrist. If you didn't want the truth about yourself as she saw it, you didn't want to schedule a session.

"Ben, don't ask me questions you don't want the answers to," she'd say. "I'm not cut out for bullshit or coddling. It's not healthy and I won't do it."

She kept me sane, got inside me. We got so we would go hours, days without talking and almost never out of anger or despair or frustration with each other. We just knew. None of that was by my choice. I would have talked my head off all the time; Grace taught me the wonder of silence, even the necessity for a civilized person to be silent, keep his damned yapping to himself. And her touch was electric to me. She knew it too, damn her. She was in charge of that. Gorgeous woman. My moonlight and my rain.

What's more her patients got better or at least learned to live with truth. She showed me my truth. I like to think I showed her some too. She loved my softness, but would not tolerate it being voiced. Once she said, "Don't cry. Don't cry, Ben!" when an old friend of ours lost her child, "if you start crying…if you cry long enough then I'll start and I won't stop. I won't ever stop."

It always made me sad that she didn't trust that I could stop her crying. She didn't trust the power of others' weaknesses. That may have been her only weakness as a wife, a friend, and a head doctor.

Cry old girl
Let that river flow through the ice
Melt it down
Melt it more
Cry those tears old as a plesiosaur
When I see the way, I'll dry you like a worn old hanky
Make you laugh through the ice
Smile at the stars.

She didn't believe it could be done, my Grace. I loved her for that too. The pain of the loss of her is like an aging scar now. I run my fingers over it. There's a kind of grotesque beauty in it like the shell of of a walnut or a snail shell… She used to tell me I looked too hard for the odd. That when the obvious was staring me in the face I'd overlook it to try to coax some parrot with a broken beak to stand on my shoulder instead of just listening to the robin's song. Okay, Grace, so I'll just say it's easier now. It ain't perfect, though.

I've cut a good path across the ice to the peninsula between Big Mud and Little Mud right across the main body of Hunter Lake. I went on snowshoes a couple times and now we're good with skis. In spots the ice has blown clear and then it's a little hairy on my 60 year old legs, ha, hairy legs, but it's fun. If the wind hits

me just right I just glide like an ice boat even up on the edges of
my skis. I feel about 15 then, full of fun and fear and hope.
        Huck has always been skeptical about the ice. He's
especially so now. He looks at me like, "Hey, there's water under
here and I like water, but I've fallen through ice before and that's
not fun." He's doing well, though he hangs back a ways, goes at his
own pace, sensible old guy, while Tom is our not so fearless scout,
going on always well ahead. He dives in the snow and rolls, more
so the colder it gets. Why I wonder? Is it some primal thing about
bathing, genetic thing about stimulating some gland? Or is it just
a hell of a good doggy time to have snow all over your face while
you're kicking all four legs in the air? He doesn't know and doesn't
seek to. That's a luxury.
        In the wake of something as simple and naturally beautiful
as ice and snow and the stars all I can find it in my heart and mind
and makeup to do is speculate, guess, analyze. I can't just be glad.
I can't just look at all the beauty and mystery and just be glad.
That's what Tom is, just a twirling ball of ears and fur and teeth and
happiness. Ain't snow grand? He says. Just grand. Lucky dog.
        The pasty I'm eating was made by the ladies at St. Ann's.
I like them…the pasties and the ladies. They don't scrimp on the
pasty meat. The rutabagas are good too and with some pepper? I
remember, right after Grace died, Kate needed a mom to help out
with the church fund raiser for the Spring production of *Midsummer
Night's Dream* that she was starring in as Titania. I went over, and
those ladies shooed me away like I was one of my labs running
amok.
        "Dr. O'Brian, don't you have some papers to grade?" old
Mrs. Frazier said to me. "Maybe some poetry to write? We've got
this handled." Kate just kind of shrugged. The ladies at St. Ann's
weren't ready for the highly evolved dad Kate wanted me to be.
Needed me to be. I'm afraid I've fallen short on that mark. Kate has
poked me about it a time or two, but never in a mean way.
        Every time I start a sentence with, "Now you girls…"
referring to women Kate's age or older she just rolls her eyes, but
eventually she grins.

I am a 20th century man. I was raised on two parents at home, sit down to the table at 6 p.m., respect your elders, honor your relatives and your ancestors, let grandma read your tea leaves, and don't give me that shit! My parents understood but did not participate in the 60's, and reviled those who lost themselves in the 70's. Mom grieved her way into the 80's while never losing a grip on her teaching job, even after she officially retired late in that decade. By the 90's she was mellowing, saying things like, "Oh don't be so hard on that boy, Ben!" And in the 0's, she was dying with Jake and Jen and Kate near her side and me saying goodbye to Grace and then joining them when that was over.

The technology which seems to be most of what is passing for history now eludes me. Though, that really isn't accurate. For something to elude a person, the person has to be pursuing it. Me? I'd rather walk on the lake. Luckily, in the Upper Peninsula of Michigan, a person can live the way I want to more than in most places in America. Everything we do in this country now seems to devolve into bad science fiction. The elections are dominated by sound bytes, and twitter and a thousand things I don't understand. Both Mike and Kate have done their best to update me, but it ends up just making me feel dated. Nope, I'm a 20th century man. And stubborn as hell. As both Kate and Grace would remind me.

Right up to her end Grace moved with the times. Texting with Mike…Michael as she called him as soon as he asked her to, no matter where he was. She rarely texted Kate, though. She rarely talked to her really. They respected each other, loved each other, but they were never chatty. Kate was right there when her mother needed her and Grace seemed to expect that. Not demand, just expect. Kate has never shown an ounce of resentment to me about her mom, or a word of regret. Not unlike Grace and me I guess, the two of them could be in the same house all day long without talking. Are they cold? No, I don't think so. I think the two of them are just sensible in a senseless world.

Many times, when Mike was younger, we'd try to goad them into getting gabby by singing silly songs, dancing around with them, even making faces. They might grin, but they wouldn't crack.

They loved us for it though, I think…but hell, I don't know.

I wish some of that would wear off on Jen. That little pistol…she's a dandy. Her business has been my business since she was 4 and I was 14. Even at 50 she's just gotta know. The little sister stereotype has a picture of her as a little girl next to it. There she is looking in at the door jam, blond pigtails hanging down, crouched on her skinny spider legs with an ear cocked towards me talking to my girlfriend. I said to my brother-in-law, Mark just last week, "Any way you can curb her enthusiasm for other people's business?" Her grinned at me as we sat there at the bakery counter drinking coffee, "In all the time you've known her, have you ever managed that?" I said, "Point taken."

She was over here with molasses cookies the other day, a whole big fucking pan of them, like I need that: 40 pounds over weight! The bastards were good though…ate them all goddamnit! There had been a big early February snow and the camp road was now exactly the way I like it: impassable. Would be for weeks now. Only way in would be to walk or ski until the melts came in March or early April. She comes over here, on this day, to camp, trudges in from the corner a quarter of a mile on snowshoes just to bring me cookies? I'm supposed to believe this is just sisterly love. The first thing she said after whipping open the door without knocking and making me drop my Emerson volume and spill my coffee over it was, "What the hell do you do in here?"

"Hello to you too."

"Seriously, what the hell. Here's some cookies."

"Like my fat ass needs that…"

"Screw you, I'll give them to Huck and Tom then."

Huck had already heard "cookies" and "Huck" and he was on it. Truthfully, he loves Jen anyway, acts like a puppy around her, the big old fool. Always liked the girls.

"Jen, what are you…"

"I just came to visit my recluse brother before he tries to off himself again…"

"You're so delicate, you know?"

"Delicacy doesn't work with you."

"Have you ever tried it? I didn't notice."

"Yes, I did. You didn't notice."

"Okay wise guy, what do you want?"

"Just to sit and talk with my big doofus brother."

"Okay, shoot."

"So…what are you up to?"

"News bulletin: I'm reading and writing poetry and walking and skiing in the snow."

"No ice fishing?"

"If Mark comes out maybe I'll cut a few holes."

"Why couldn't we cut a few holes?"

"Do you want to cut a few holes?"

"Hell no…"

"Then why would you…"

"Because of the assumptions you make! For all your high fallutin' pretense as the poet laureate of the U.P. and a college professor…"

"Never claimed the first retired from the second…"

"…you're just another guy making assumptions about what women…like and…"

"Have you ever ice fished?"

"Yes! I've been out there a bunch of times with you…"

"That's not what I asked. I asked if you've ever ice fished, and the answer is no. You've sat by me as I ice fished playing 25,000 questions, jabbering away so no self respecting fish would come within…"

"I was just a little girl…"

"And that's the last time you ice fished! I'm not making sexist assumptions about women, I'm making logical assumptions about you, you skulking little sneak! And don't try to hide behind that plate of cookies, I know why you're here."

"Because I love you and I worry about you…"

"Okay…I don't mean to be harsh. Sorry. I know that's true and I appreciate that, but…"

"What else is there? My big brother likes to go off by himself and sometimes he goes OFF when he's by himself…"

"Okay. Okay. I love you too. But are you sure you're not just trying to get the scoop?"

"I retired as a newspaper reporter two years ago…"

"But you didn't retire from getting the scoop. And there's still your gossip column."

"Local news."

"Fine, but your local news column is called 'The Scoop'."

"Okay. Okay. Granted. You're pissed at me and you're cranky as hell generally, so I know you're okay. Huck's telling me not to worry, and Tom doesn't look the worse for wear, so I'll let you go."

"Okay then…"

"When do you want the next batch?"

"When hell freezes over! I won't eat these."

"Uh huh…See you in a few days."

That was Thursday. It's Monday morning and they're gone. Damn her for being right.

We're a comedy team, Jen and I, but I don't think either of us mean to be. Jen's a serious person when she's not around me. She was a good reporter, a fine community theatre actress, but she becomes my sneaky little sister whenever she's around me. And I become a cranky old bastard, big brother when I'm around her. And…she's right. She was one of the main lights that got me through the dark times after Grace. I should be nicer to her. I doubt I will be, though.

That just leaves my asshole brother Jake. Well, not really an asshole… An ass, though, and hard to figure. I haven't thought about him in a while. He slips my mind because he's so distant, as in distance. I'm not even really sure what he does. He's a lawyer for the government, and he travels to third world countries helping them set up systems of laws as near as I can figure out. Where is he now? You know, I don't know…the Eastern Block somewhere. There never were any flies on him. He's been moving since he was two. He always has kept his own counsel too. Mom used to just look at him and smile. Dad loved watching him on the field and court. Jesus he was good. Delicate, delicate wrist flick and nothing but net even at age 11. So sad Dad didn't get to see him after that. Damned shame. That delicacy, artistic coordination. That's what I remember about him most. I was a pounder and a hacker on the basketball court, but he just flowed. Knew where everybody was. All state point guard, lightening quick reflexes. And the one time I had him out hunting with me, he shot ducks out of the air like he was at the carnival shooting gallery. Violation of the hunter's code: never be a better shot than your host. Gifted. Just gifted that way. Never married. Now he's 57. Lots of girls around him always. He's the looker, with Dad's dark eyes and hair and that slim build he's maintained. All that comes to me about him, whenever I see him is what he always says when I see him at weddings and funerals and sometimes holidays: "shiny".

"How goes it, Jake?"

"Shiny." And then he shoots Dad's crooked grin my way. He's just saying, I'm okay Ben. Always was, always will be, don't worry. And that's all he wants me to know. I've seen he and Jen huddled in corners talking lots of times, but for me it's just "Shiny." Bugs me a little. Now who's trying to get the scoop?

That wolf keeps coming back to me. He's trying to become a metaphor for something. Rather, I'm trying to make him one. He's alone like, Jake… or me, Jen would argue. Kate knows better. She knows how much I need others, though I deliberately seek to be away. And then I stay away too long. And that's when it's bad. Maybe Jen does get me. The wolf, though… He's big. He's searching for sustenance. He's in the moment because he has to be, though he seems contemplative too, at least he was when he saw Huck, Tom, and me. Those eyes looked us over. Or maybe he just gave us a good sniff. What does a wolf think? There's always a chance of anthropomorphizing animals, as I do too often with Huck and Tom, but is it so different? I mean I can't count the times that Huck has "given me the paw". He'll walk up to me and slap that massive right bear paw of his, he's right pawed, on my knee. If I remove it, he just does it again, as many times as necessary until he delivers his message. "I'm hungry, I need a walk. You're thinking too hard. What the hell are you doing?" There's no way in the world that's not what he means. Seems human, but maybe not. Maybe we're just so full of ourselves that a lot of things we think are human are merely sentient.

Really, is it so different? At a basic primal level it can't be, and beyond that? What higher levels if any, do they attain in their processes? What are higher levels? Certainly he understands way more about smell than I do, and sees better at night. His hearing is certainly better, and his stamina. What does he do with those gifts? Of what use are they?

We can't know
We can't no
Without knowing
We poo poo all the critters
Figure they don't know shit
But they do
They really know shit
Lots of shit we don't
Some we wouldn't want to
Wolves and coyotes
Squirrels and chippies
Shape shifting in the shadows
Tree to tree
Life to life
Passing on in grunts and whines
What all our long talks with wine soaked brain cells
Won't tell
Tell me true
How well do you know the nearest
Fur bearer to you?

That's pretty silly. Is that okay? I mean I don't want to come off like Ogden Nash. I always run the risk of anthropomorphizing animals in my life I'm always getting told that my poetry is so spiritual. I hate that. Maybe because it sounds pretentious. I don't want to be pretentious. My old poetry professor used to look at my poetry, shake his head and say, "There's that tone again." And then he wouldn't tell me how not to have it. I think he was saying my poetry was pedantic. But certainly Robert Frost was pedantic, "Two roads diverged in a yellow wood..." "Whose woods these are I think I know..." If you tell somebody something you sound Pedantic. "Because I could not stop for death"... Pedantic. "My mistress' eyes are nothing like the sun" playful but pedantic. "I write in the clear sun, in the teeming street, at full sea tide, in a place where I can sing..." Pedantic! I wonder if ol' B. W. my teacher, thought I hadn't earned it and so shouldn't be pedantic, or if he thought nobody should ever be. It's an interesting question. And I've heard young writers express the idea that your writing should never show you to be certain of anything, never judgmental about anything. Okay, so what if you are certain? What if you are even certain that something is wrong or right ("the time was neither wrong nor right")? Should a poet, a writer then pretend to still be uncertain? Isn't that pretense? Isn't that adopting a false tone of uncertainty? Maybe it's okay to say anything so long as you don't sound certain. That's just fashion then isn't it? It reminds me of the kids, not so many around these days, mostly they speak in monotone, who used to phrase every statement? Like a question? They were certainly following ol' B.W.'s dictum. I respected my professor very much and loved his poetry, which was, rarely pedantic. I have this nagging suspicion that he was right about me. That pisses me off because I don't know how to write any other way.

Shit.

Chapter 2
Grace Now

He gets lost. That's what he does, Dear soul; he gets lost. That is the thing the Spheres love most about him. Those who are lost can be found. Can find out. Can grow. It's the daring of being lost They love I think. Rarely once a soul is old can it be lost without its own permission. The young ones get lost, are lost, almost all the time and are innocent of the knowledge. That's another story. This time my Ben is out in the snow, out on the ice, with those dear…dogs. *They're* not lost. They're never lost. They are more tied to it, unblinded by troublesome, lovely, disquieting, intellect. They are in touch, in tune. That older one, Huck he's called, he just hums with connections. Rare Rare. He's a true heart and is conscious too. He's a rare mixture for that….ha…breed. But my Ben, soon not just *my* Ben, is lost. He's sad. The Spheres love the lost. When I was my other I, I loved Ben's sadness most. To be alive and not to be sad much of the time, is to be truly lost, or unconscious. There's so much they hurt about, the good ones. I wonder…well, no I don't. I never wonder any more…none of us do. We're all face to Face now. We're all Known. There's just the music, the music. Still, I am not a conscious one now. Not in that other sense, though one of their… psychiatrists…huh…that other I of me was one of those…would probably say that what I am becoming is a kind of disembodied consciousness. A ghost maybe, except I'm the opposite of that. I'm not wandering. I'm not wondering. There's no unfinished business.

I'm quite fulfilled where I am…yet I am waiting. Waiting not to be able to look and listen. Waiting to blend. I'm not haunting or haunted. Ha, that's not our gig.

Ah…anyway…he gets lost. My old Ben. Funny, but his kind of lost is closer to being found. He'll have very little trouble when he gets here. Ha, unless he causes it himself, which I can see he will, just to be difficult, hanging on to that last vestige of ego. He's been at the crossroads a long time. Like that poet…Frost he was called…who wrote the poem about the birches, about not wanting to really let go, but wanting just a hint. Just a hint. That happens in life down there sometimes. Sometimes it happens because it's supposed to, but if it's something you're trying for all the time, joining groups and cults and a million and one little float-about societies, it's really just a kind of celestial voyeurism. Not much good for anything, but a higher thrill. And those groups are all too often about only that, a thrill, a need to be the one who comes back to Socrate's and Plato's cave with the knowledge of the upper world, the sun. When people do that, then it's just about ego, and will cancel out in the selfish seeking whatever gains might be made in some cosmic realization. Ego plays only a negative role here. But Ben has stood at that solid crossroad for so long, become almost a gatekeeper there, just because that's who he is, that he'll be used to this feeling that subsides, that is subsiding in me. He'll be a little scared, but not as much as most. He's been lost. He's been found. And now he's out on the…ice, out in the…snow.

Nouns they used to call those. Still do, I guess. They haven't stopped just because I'm not fully there. Ego. Ego. It hangs on… Nouns are the first things that go. They are the most solid. Even the…ideas. There's lots to hang your hat on down there. Here there are no hats, no hangers, no need for either. No tops, no bottoms, only…only big spherical mirrors that sing. Or maybe it's more like being inside spherical mirrors that… Ha. That's not it really, actually it's way off, probably further than not knowing at all, no point in even trying to describe in a place that's not a place. The moment you try to pin It down in a concrete description it all becomes more abstract and complex. And this itself is false, because It's all very simple. There are no details to describe; there are no general impressions, all is unspecific and completely specific. One, one, one, and the music, one glorious note and all notes, other worldly, otherwordly, not worldly or wordy, not and so totally so. Ha, ha, ha. No way…but it's as close as I can come as any can come, with words, words words. That's a quote from something…something Ben dearly loves…Shakespeare. *Hamlet*. Shakespeare: there was a lot of Here in him even before he came. He was always standing at this crossroads, from the day he was born.

Dear Ben. Poor Ben. The good Dr. O'Brian. "The Doofus" as Jen calls him. I do so love him. Sad… that that will be gone soon too. But only sad in the way of Earth. In the way of not knowing. So lovely not to know, as near as I can recall. So awful. They love the temporal there. They love the impermanence. They love the Fall. And to love the Fall in the North, in the…Upper Peninsula of Michigan…(Ha, so strange to remember something so specific, so completely imaginary yet real). To love the Fall there is to love a moment. Just a moment in a whole year. Multi-colored leaves and crisp air. Oh, I can smell it. That's not good really, but it is lovely. They love the Fall. The Fall from grace, like Lucifer's, which is what the temporal is. No, that doesn't mean they're demonic. It means they're Earthly humans. They are given choices and they accept them consciously or unconsciously. They don't see yet that there really are no choices, because choices imply that something is about to happen or something has happened, that one thing happens after another and we have to make selections of what we will do and what we won't do within that frame. Here we know that this is all illusion. Not that there are no choices, but that all choices are the same choice ultimately, or presently and that because this is so, choices are actually illusion. I know…riddles…I'm talking in riddles. I'm sorry. There's really no other way. Poets try to explain that to people too. Many never get it. Or don't pay close enough attention to. That's it, really, paying attention until you don't have to, until it becomes intrinsic in every breath…Oh…ha…riddles again.

Anyway, they love the mortal down there and cry for it. So sad to think that love, even my individual love for Ben will soon be gone. Not love general. That won't be gone. That always is. That's all there is. Love specific is what goes. We learn that love specific is disingenuous eventually. To love one more than others is terrestrial love. It's ha, undemocratic. To love one who is hateful, that is more the direction that truly lives here. To love someone first out of pity for their being hateful. Then just to love them without even seeing what is evil, but only the good slice. To recognize that good and evil are judgements made by terrestrial judges, and that acts of true evil are to be pitied, not abhorred because, though such base acts reverberate and devastate even here, their final results are so very temporal, like nearly everything on Earth. As in the poem, Evil looks into the cosmos and sees "…rank on rank, The army of unalterable law…" of eternal divine love. All things on Earth are temporal, everything but love and here that love transcends and becomes all, and nothing else has true existence. And that is the way where Ben is on Earth as well. It's there in every thunderstorm and sunrise, rock and flower, but no one there is capable of seeing that truth for long. It's just too much. It's just too good. They are frightened by the light like the prisoners of that cave. I have to keep reminding myself of that. Or perhaps I have to forget to remind myself of that so often that there becomes nothing to remind myself of. No moments past. No moments to come. Nothing to regret, anticipate or remember. Only the now.

      Their love, their best love, like mine and Ben's or Ben and Jen's, is a scent of this, of here. It's the best thing. He feels it and disbelieves it. He is half seduced, like so many other bright ones that it's all scents and genomes and pheromones and firing synapses. They come to believe, sad creatures, that you could put love into a Petri dish and separate its parts. What is ultimately true is beyond the kind of science they know so far, though they have done wonders, they suffer by the necessity, and it is a necessity for now, of making everything too hard, too complex. It will be necessary to push this complexity until it becomes simplicity as has been done so many other times which are all the one time. Between the study and the realization there is no time, because THERE IS NO TIME, but the illusion of extended study for minutes, hours, days, weeks, months, years eons is absolutely necessary so that the moment can be the moment of realization: the best moment, which is every moment, which is now and then and forever. Deep in his seduction by the material, Ben ponders love which is life. This is the first mistake all thinking people make. I certainly made it. Only now, which is forever, do I realize that there's nothing to ponder. It just is. And once you fully perceive, you know. Sadly though, and sadness is temporal too, but has a sweetness that is hard to resist, you can only truly perceive that love is truly all, for moments there. It's all you can grasp and it is elusive even in the grasping. But in those moments what wonder! Ben has had several of those moments, but like everyone there always forgets how they were. Those wonderful moments when there's nothing to wonder about. Everything, every time, every place, every person just is. All the things you think? They're true and totally wrong also. There is no right or wrong, this or that, mission or omission. In deep, Ben knows this already. He knows. He knows. And he just can't admit. He can't admit the idea into his consciousness. It's too big and too small, enormous and infinitesimal, so far beyond and within idea or concept that you can't even see those things from here. He knows that too, but just can't, just can't make it work. He loves the Earth. He loves his senses. He feels so hard. That's why he gets so completely lost. Like now. He's always looking and so he ventures out and loses himself within.

Years from now, ha, I was forgetting what that means "years". There are no years really. When Ben gets here I'll be able to love him specifically. Rather, I am able to love him specifically, until...ha, there's no until either...so hard using temporal language to describe the eternal that is momentary. The one moment. The Only moment. The big bang and before, the big bust and after... all the moments the seconds of love and terror, boredom and excitement, banality and ecstasy... Anyway, in that time and space which is now and here, Ben won't need my special, specific love, and I'll stop, turn from him, but not really. I'll have faces for everyone and everything including him, and no faces at all. It won't be after, it won't be before. It will be now. I know, hard to follow, but it won't be. Anyway, there, where there's time, when he confesses this day to Jen, this silly, dangerous going out into a blizzard, she'll say, "Who does that? Who goes out on the ice in a whiteout? You wanted to 'know it'? Well, I guess you know it now! You're lucky you didn't KNOW your fingers off or your toes. Or your dick, you doofus! Hey, you didn't did you… No? Well, there's that. Promise me you'll never do that again, and I'll promise never to tell anyone you did it."

And he will promise, and he won't do it again, and unlike any other time in her life, Jen will never tell a living soul about it. Resisting something that delicious for a silly story teller, like Jen? Now that's love! I do love what they are together so much. It shines so. It glimmers even here. I look at it sometimes, all the time, two souls, two spirits so in sync are so rare. And what's funny is they think they're galaxies apart. They're both tugging on the same rope, making the battle which is a dance. On this the spheres and I agree completely. As if I could ever do anything else but agree. As if there were any reason to. Soon we'll agree on everything. We do agree on everything already, just a little more has to go. A little more of that other I. I can see it. I can see it. I am it. I'm there. And I'm not. No contradiction, only harmony, that's the song.

My little bit to go is Ben. He has to let go from the other end. He has to quit wishing me alive again. He has to help me, and he is trying, but it's so hard from that end and we were so close. He has a ways to go, but something's coming. Something's almost here. It is here, but I can't quite make it out. Jen will be a part of it, and my darling Kate, and dear Michael. And Mark and that rascal Jake.

Oh Ben. Oh Ben. He knew the storm was coming and he skiied out there with those dogs, out into the night. He'd read a forecast that the storm would end about 9 p.m. and then all would be clear. He wanted to see that, see the stars come out of the clouds in the darkness. And he'd been berating himself for his fear of going out under the stars. The fear that the wolf might come. And the wolf does come, but he's no danger. Not the wolf, not the metaphor. He's just part of it all. He's a very necessary part. So Ben headed out just as it started to snow heavily and he got out there, and he kept walking all down the lake. The little dog wandering about, the old dog staying close, so close. He loves Ben so. Silly man didn't have a compass or matches. My old self would have said that was intentional, that some of that suicide instinct was still hanging on from that other time, but it isn't so. It's a matter of fulfilling what must be and Ben knows this at some level. At this level that's only now developing in him. Sometimes I can almost see him here. Sometimes, just for instants that are eternities he's here and he holds my old hand.

He went out into that storm and when he turned around the snow had come in a wall of white and the darkness was all around and his young soul part cried out, and he turned again three times and he didn't know the way home. He followed Huck for a while, and of course the old dog was headed the right way, the only way he knows, but that ego, that human ego wouldn't let him trust and time, that ultimate illusion, seemed to be roaring past, it seemed hours, days, and finally he ended up heading for a shore, and he found a deadfall and got in under there with the dogs. And they were all warm. Sweet. So sweet. And worry mostly went away and he slept. When he woke, he was shaking and frightened so frightened and that made the shaking bigger, he thought life threatening, still thinks so, but he looked out and he could see the stars, and the moon, the milky way and he said, "Wow!" the way he does. And then the dear, silly man fell asleep again.

Ben's sense of wonder may be the thing I love most about him. The sense of wonder which is tied with the sadness in a continuum that isn't one. All one. All one. And when he woke up in the morning, he walked shaking and quaking back to the warm camp and lit a fire and laughed at himself. And then, for days, weeks after he was "so damned glad to be alive" everything was a miracle, as it most certainly is, and then that faded, because it has to, because that's the way it is. People, as Frost says, have to "turn to their affairs."

Old Ben. Dear Ben. My love. I'm going. I'm going. You'll be lost and then you'll find me. Oh, but first…first they'll be more fun, more love, more life with all the sad and happy and ecstatic and banal. Life on Earth isn't this, but, it ain't bad. And something really sweet in that Earth way is coming for Ben.

And now he's warm. Now he's warm and the sun is fully up and he's drinking red wine and the fire is crackling. So seductive, the world. It loves to have you part of it. And where I am is not about detachment from all that, it's about going out to go back to feel it all deeper, to know that even the best of the physical is only essence. If we could sense in every moment everything that's there, we wouldn't need all this changing, this transformation, this evolution which endlessly evolves. We could just be in time out of time in space out of space in love always with the stars and the dirt and the spheres within spheres within spheres that burst and cry and sing and roar and squeak and drone and hum and clatter and ring and rush out into all this great expanse of fully realized life love and ether light that wills and won'ts and ushers us into ever bigger and smaller and synchronicity of all the impossible inevitabilities beyond the stars, beyond even the faintest thought of them.

So, he's warm. On Earth. In the embrace of it really, with all the great good and unnoticed darkness that pervades all there. And glad to be alive. Reborn. Yet again. By the fire. Earthbound for now. My Ben. And very, very glad to be so. Let's leave him there.

Chapter 3
Near Death
The View from the Trees

I was so happy! Joyous really, and make that have a religious connotation if you like. When my eyes opened after that blizzard, huddled between the dogs, my guys, under that deadfall... joyous! That's it. I saw the stars stretched out down the sky and I was in them, part of them, but I was here too. I was half awake, maybe, I don't know. I felt like I was all of it, Earth, stars, the snow, the cold, the dogs just one thing. I felt Grace was so close to me. My Gracie, all part of it too. So real. It was real. And then I must have fallen asleep, stupid really, maybe even dangerous, but somehow it didn't seem so. At some level I knew I'd wake up again. And when I came around again, the day had broken. A day I thought, when I was in that bone cold blizzard, I would never see. I had been so cold, so cold, a cold that defines cold forever. In the days since then at the mere hint of cold I have felt an almost physical rush back to those moments, when I really couldn't feel my hands, when I could tell I still had feet only by looking down and seeing my skis sliding in my headlamp through the wind driven flakes. I don't ever want to be that cold again, because its memory has lived long after its actual physical danger and I think that's going to be the way from now on every time the thermometer dips. To be lost in the blizzard in that awful cold and driving wind with no compass and no matches like a damned fool. It was just a stupid thing to do, to go out there to prove myself like I was an idiot 18-year-old who thought he was bulletproof instead of this all too mortal old man with definite feet of clay. But the joy at opening my eyes once to all those mighty stars and then to the dawn and being alive and well, drowned the shame out completely. I was alive damnit! Huck didn't want to move, Tom sprang out of there, wagging his whole body, *a game, a game, another day*, he seemed to say as he always does and I followed him all creaking joints and tears. I prayed right then, in the old Catholic school boy way, right down on my knees in the snow.

Joy, pure joy. Thank you. Thank you. Thank you Jesus, Jehovah, Vishnu, Shiva, Atman, Allah, Oversoul. The sun was breaking over my right shoulder and shadows were falling between the leafless hardwoods and the pine boughs. A gray squirrel sprang up on a branch six feet away chattering in front of me as I knelt.

"Hello, Bushy!" I said. "It's a damned fine day!" He chattered once, an obvious curse, (I think squirrels only speak in curse words) then bolted into the higher branches. I watched him go. I was smiling like an idiot.

Only hours before I'd been frozen with pure abject terror and low body temperature. *I'm going to die. I'm going to die.* Amazing fact bouncing around my skull hopping from neuron to neuron body and mind rebelling, working to prevent it, but it just kept getting colder. So logical, so coldly logical. If your body temp gets to a certain point…systems shut down, then there is a dreamless sleep that fades to what? For me the most terrifying thing, the one that haunts me at such moments, is that there might be nothing. Nothing at all. And then I have the argument with the other voice, the one that always says, *oh Ben you know that's not true. There certainly, certainly is something and you know that you know that. This is just a game you play to scare yourself. A spiritual rollercoaster you like to ride: The Agnostic Express, that takes you in and out of tunnels ups and downs and round about and loop the loops. So fun to ride, and when you get tired of the thrill you'll see how silly it all was.* Hard to argue with that voice. It's so pedantic. So wise. So sure of itself. Maybe that's the one that gets into my poetry. I have to admit, at times I'm very grateful for it, that certitude. It thumbs its nose at Matthew Arnold and his beautiful, bleak poem *Dover Beach*. Anyway, there in the snow I kept getting more frightened *Hail Mary full of grace…Grace…Gracie…*and then the dogs calmly breathing in and out. I tried to synchronize with them, slower, slower, jumped up in panic a few times: *This is what happens! This is what happens just before you freeze!*, but then I didn't feel cold anymore and there were those lovely stars, and then it was now. So very now.

> *"Oh God*
> *"How little I know," I prayed in that 3 a.m. nightmare*
> *just before those gorgeous stars*
> *"And know least in what I think I know*
> *"Ignorance is a blast*
> *"Knowing is scary as hell*
> *"Let me live*
> *"Let me live*
> *"Let me live"*

And now You have let me live. Breathe in and out. Head back to camp. Start a fire. Smell the sunrise. Talk to my beautiful brilliant daughter, my holy fool son on a goddamned cell phone. What a joy! What pure joy to be part of the material and the transcendent all at once, to know that there is a purpose. There is a meaning. There is meaning just in being known by the folks that love you, even by the folks who are only acquaintances. What can you do for them? What can you show them before you pass on to whatever comes after. That's the point. That's always been the point. Learn as much as you can and give comfort, for God's sake give comfort! We were placed here to urge others on, pat other backs. Why does it take this? Why does it always take facing what it would be like not to be able to help anyone, least of all ourselves, to make us realize that it's so good just to be alive, to have the opportunity to be of use?

Sadly, it never lasts. Even as I'm feeling this I know that it never lasts. I can see it right now, this thing that is light and ashes in the fire and the pop of good wood and the family pictures on the wall and my children's voices on the phone and it all just takes me up into those stars, deeper into the fire. I pet my wonderful simple dogs who in some ways must exist in this way, this fully informed, fully alive way all the time. It's second nature. There's no thinking about it, considering whether it's true. It's true. It just is. They are accepting of the incredible because it is not incredible to them. I need to work so hard to realize the extraordinary in the ordinary; I have to continually go through all kinds of spiritual calisthenics, sometimes for years at a time just to get a glimpse of it. I have to have my life in danger before I can see the wonder of a shimmering wake of stars and a popping fire and a loving voice on the phone.

A few moments ago I discovered a cooler outside the back door which had once been filled with ice during duck season. Then, after I forgot the cooler behind the door, it became melt water on a warm day some time in October. Still forgotten until this moment in February, the melt water became, in the three months since, a block of ice. Moments ago, I brought it inside and ran hot water in the cooler in the sink to melt it down. When the block loosened, I took it out of the cooler and set it in the sink continuing to run hot water over it. Before I knew it, I had become fascinated with the journey of the water from ice block to a stream of water flowing down the drain. And only on this morning would the next thing have occurred:

> *Just a change*
> *another change*
> *small change*
> *this death.*
> *Water becomes ice, becomes water, becomes ice.*

> *Presto, change-o*
> *Abracadabra*
> *In the name of the Father*
> *and of the Son*
> *and of the Holy Spirit*

of life and water and ice.

We alter on Your altar and off.
We drain out and fill up.
We freeze and flow.

And all changes
especially death
are just this small change.

What we are, we are forever
in any way that matters:
an essence of fires and waters
flitting free from any form
we imprison ourselves within.

All is temporal but the All we are always.

Hop in
there's plenty of room in this translucent star car.
Don't worry
we aren't going very far
just a skip and a jump
over the hump and back
just around the block from our Always home.

This universe is really small
and everything changes all the time
into smiles wider than Orion's Belt.

Small change
small change.
Ice becomes water.
Life becomes death.
Forming into formless
down the drain

out again and back in the game.

All the way out to sea and back
we're in our own country
that's everywhere,
everyone.

Change.
Change in our universal pocket
clanking, squeaking
crunching, and sploshing.

You can't take what won't stop
seriously.
It's just a funny howdy do.
How do we do it?

We don't.

This is a bigger brush stroke
that we don't have enough paint for.
A metaphor that writes itself
Small change.
Small change.

Life into your death.
Ice in your drink.
Water later
and ice again.
Small
change.
Change
small.
What's once is for all.

Well, I don't know if that's pedantic or just loony. What's really funny is I don't care. I'm in this lovely lighted cloud and everything seems pretty marvelous. I've a man on the drawbridge between life and death and there's a party on both sides. One side is a green and earthy gathering, maybe a wedding feast, full of dark beer, wine, fine roast wild duck, fish gumbo, and laughing voices. Everyone is red faced from the cold, but standing by a rosy fire. There are young people and old at this gathering and it's full of life.

The other end is home to ethereal music and a permanent light that is a color I've never seen before. It's kind of what gold and silver mixed want to be when they grow up. And the music just keeps going and it has words. Wonderful words I don't understand. Words that would be cheapened by my conventional understanding. Chimes and friendly roars, and almost goofy grunts and long, twisting elliptical words. And figures there shimmering ethereal and still, so still. There's a dignity to the sound and stillness in that direction: the essence of pure thought and feeling. Life that is beyond life, the negation and epitome of all our fondest dreams. One, one, one. A single note brings it to a crescendo, and then it fades away on the morning wind.

I'm the guy, the lucky guy on this bridge who gets to look both ways. I get to see both ways. And for once I don't have to choose. I can just be here with my living and dead loves and bathe in the light and twilight of all of it: my Gracie, my goofy dogs, my kid's questions, my sister's taunts, my friends' jokes, my father's slow friendly advice, my mother's demands and commands and working hands, and all the words and books and walks I love. It's all here, right now. Now on the bridge between. I don't have to choose. I can just stay. And for now, for now, that's what I'm going to do. Talk later.

Chapter 4
Near Death
Boom!

He was no one without her. He woke up realizing this. She was 15 years gone and he was only now getting that he'd been missing his identity without Grace all that time. Yet it wasn't quite that. He still had personality, likes, dislikes, beliefs, satisfaction, frustration, anger, happiness. He was still loved. He still loved. He was an entity having impact on the earth, in both nature, and society. Yet in his heart he felt an alienation, a disjointed, diffuse feeling, as though he were not quite real, as though she were the vessel that gave him shape. That was it. He had gone from solid when she lived, to fluid as she died, slowly defusing to a nebulous…what was the word…"inert" gas. He was in an existential gaseous state now. There was no Ben O'Brian without Grace Houseman-O'Brian. He was this vague state of love, hate, sadness, and joy floating about rooms and relationships with loved ones and strangers, but never engaging, committing, or creating through his own decisions and actions.

Gaseous.

5:05 a.m. Still lying in the lower bunk in the back of the camp, just a day after his survival through the blizzard, he laughed aloud. At the sound, Tom and Huck, in their cedar bag dog beds, between the outer wall of the camp and the sideboard of the bed, shifted and raised their heads.

What's up?

Still laughing, Ben looked over at their glimmering eyes in the dark and said, "I'm gaseous guys! I'm an old fart!"

Boom!

Or not quite boom.

Rattle. Compression. Tremor. Release. A rushing out of pressure powerful enough to take his breath away and shake the whole damned camp.

The dogs were alert, alarmed.

What the hell just happened?

"Something big…"

He stumbled his way out from under the upper bunk and feeling odd, old, shaken, staggered towards the wall nearest the doorway, then wondered if getting out from under cover was a good idea. He stood there for five seconds taking inventory.

He thought: *Now this thing that has happened; has it happened to the whole cabin or just me?*

He counted to ten silently, listening. It hadn't been like a gun shot. It was much louder, more deeply encompassing, not a crack, a low bass explosion. Gods beneath the earth stuff. Zeus or Odin making a pronouncement. He'd never been in an earthquake, but it seemed of nearly such magnitude. Nothing else had exploded. Inside him or outside him. The dogs stood looking up at him, questions written on their faces.

What now boss?

"Okay, guys, I get it. It definitely isn't just me. Let's go see what the hell it is, eh?"

He pulled on his sweatpants and grabbed an old fisherman's sweater from the shelf, then headed for the front door turning on lights as he went. Near the door he put his bare feet into his laceless rubber swamper boots. He went out into the night. The cold air, 10 degrees at most, was a shock this early, but Tom was bouncing around. Huck, clearly sensing something wrong hung close to Ben.

Feeling the old dog get closer to him, intentionally rub against his leg as they walked, Ben thought of how it was always this way with Huck.

Like the time when he was younger and we were walking behind the lake along the logging road in the stand of beeches and suddenly that moose was right in my face as I came around a corner. I stood there in shock. She looked up at me, pawed the ground once. No idea what to do. And here came Huck, who had been smelling something a few steps back, maybe the moose itself. And suddenly he was right in her face and she turned, which wasn't easy for her, like a Greyhound bus working into a parking space, and ran for her life into the woods. God, what a dog!

God, what are we going to find in this basement?

They walked the few steps down hill to the basement door. Looking up he spotted clear cold stars. Still there.

So this wasn't a cosmic event.

In the half light something looked strange about the mass of the multi-paned front basement window. It seemed somehow, bent, stars and the moon were shining off the panes at odd angles. He opened the basement door and turned on the light wondering in that instant if it was safe to do so. Apparently, it was. On the top of the massive old oil furnace the detached business end of a ramrod standing vertical in an old, white, broken coffee cup, burned like a small candle. The metal front door of the furnace lay on the floor. All of the furnace piping, which had extended up towards the first floor, lay twisted on the floor as well. Soot from the furnace was everywhere. Ben looked back towards the front window. The whole six foot high, ten foot wide window framework was pushed out at the center, converted into an arrow pointing towards the lake. There was a good deal of glass scattered on the floor.

"Jesus Christ…"

He stood looking around for a moment once again and realized the furnace had exploded, or at least released a hell of a lot of pressure. He walked to where the ramrod head lay burning and blew it out.

"It's not even my birthday."

Then Ben walked to the switchbox and turned the power off to the furnace, though he wondered what possible difference it could make now.

He would call someone in the morning. This was clearly way beyond his expertise, which stopped at imperfectly pounding nails and badly painting trim. Now what? He stood in minor shock for half a minute until Huck gave a little whining groan.

Keep movin' boss.

Right. So, now he needed to stoke the fire. He went back up the hill to the upstairs, shutting off the basement light and shutting the door, though anything that wanted to get in there today would have easy access through the reformed window hole. He went inside at the front door followed by the dogs. He went to the woodbox and systematically stoked the fire.

He stood staring at it for a moment. Tears were suddenly in his eyes. It was partly fear, but it was also a strange kind of amusement.

How many bullets am I going to dodge? That's two in 48 hours! What lesson am I being sent? I guess maybe I better prepare to live for a while, because apparently it isn't my time to die yet.

Living. What a concept!

"Boys," he said to the dogs, "let's go for a ski in honor of another near death experience."

Huck was slowly wagging his tail, his veiled lids seeming to express bemusement for the ten thousandth time. "Crazy old man," Ben said in the imagined voice of Huck, "I got your back." The tail wagged harder.

Half an hour later three quarters of the way to the channel he felt as though he were floating. He'd looked back at the camp several times. At first he could still pick up the moon shining weirdly off the broken glass in the basement window. Something. Something happening there. Then he'd looked away and moved on. None of it seemed real. He watched the dogs going about their business as though nothing had happened: Huck plodding along, nose coming up occasionally, to check on him. Tom bouncing around everywhere, running to shore, finding sticks, coming back, trying to entice Huck, who hardly noticed Tom's efforts, into chasing him.

A poem took shape in Ben's head:

I almost died.
Then, I almost died again.
The family would have cried.
Twice
They almost all were crying.
Why do I place myself between the magnet and the metal
In these multiple polarized moments?
Do I suppose some gentle hand will stay the force of Earth?
Do I suppose the course of life is planned, like on a map?
That I hold its paper folds in my own hands
And I've got miles galore ahead?

I could have been dead.
I could have been dead again.
Frozen to the core in a forest.
or
Burned to a crisp in bed.

Instead,
I'm sliding along on my silly skis.
Looking up at my 60th year of cold blue sky.

I tell myself little lies that add up,
Just so not to see the almost
Hosts of calamities all along my road.

I just ski.

I ski.
I whistle.
I wheeze.
I spit.

I tell myself my passing through and over pleases the wind and
frozen water.

I take my son and daughter, my sneaky sister and distant brother
All for granted.

I seem to ease my way into and out of every day.
I worry vacant lots, but not correctly.

Worry is just a happy pastime to so far deathless me.

There's no permanent pain.

Time passing.
Time passing.

Did I almost die?
So I did, but I didn't this time either.
So,
I ski,
I ski,
I ski.

He skied near to the channel where Tom was drinking and backing away from the breaking ice at water's edge, tail wagging the whole time. The young dog occasionally looked up as Ben and Huck approached.

"No wolf today, fellas."

Ben scanned the horizon of the lake to be sure. He would have to call Dale at the furnace place in Hunter in a couple hours. Probably wasn't worth fixing the damned old furnace. Dad had put it in with Dale's grandfather, what, 50 years ago. Who knows how long that old furnace had been working out in Dale's family's company out building before it came to the camp. The damned thing was probably 70 years old anyway. Might almost be preserving an historical monument if he fixed it.

"Wonder if there's any public funds for the restoration?" Ben asked Huck. Huck looked up at Ben for a moment, then over towards Tom, who ran by obliviously with an enormous and gnarled piece of driftwood.

Dawn. He took off his skis and stuck them vertically with his poles in a bank of drifted snow. He sat down right on the edge of the water facing east to watch the sun come up.

"Warming up. Can't be colder than 28, 29 degrees."

There was an open patch of beach sand beneath his left knee. In the growing light he could see a tiny sunfish or "pumpkin seed" as they called them locally, perhaps an inch long, lying very still on the bank. Despite the fact that it was clearly dead, he deliberately took off his right glove in that cold air, picked it up by the tail and gently placed it in the shallows on the east end of the channel.

"Burial at sea."

Instantly, it swam away and disappeared in the tiny weeds and bits of drift wood floating in the current.

"I'll be damned!"

Has God suddenly cancelled death, or is it just me?

He laughed out loud his face creased with amazement. He hugged Huck close to him, kissing the old dog on the top of his bony head.

"We're alive buddy. We're alive! And we're here for a while. What are we going to do?"

Has God cancelled death or is it just me?
Just me living,
Just me staying to give back
To the trees and the stars
The lively little fish
And the walkers of the woods
All the joy they've sent my way?
Today I'll be happy with good reason.
In this dark season light has come back to me.
I have a right to be happy in good company
With this smiling cosmos.
I am compelled to say joyous things.
"The day goes well."

"The day goes well."
The frozen bell of mourning morning,
Unexpected, Uncalled,
Announces this ecstatic joy of life.
Whether it's just me now,
Or always God,
Death stays away today.
Summoning in His place
Some bright Truth.
That's true for always.

As the sun came up Ben O'Brian laughed hard out loud. He started tossing sticks for Tom who rushed back and forth in and out of the frigid water. He had to keep hugging Huck close over and over to keep him from chasing the younger dog.

"Let's not get carried away, bud, you're too old for that water!"

He was no one without her, but even in this gaseous state, wandering out here in the ether 15 years after his wife had gone, with no real plans, no real focus, life was still good. Life was still going on.

"I get the message."

There's a reason I need to live. Something is coming.

He suddenly knew this to be true as certainly as he knew the cold of the night before or the feel of Huck's rough coat between the bare and chilly fingers of his right hand. Something was definitely coming.

Seems childish to believe that, but I know it's true.

He remembered waking up in his dorm room all those years ago… How many? Good lord…41 years ago. Forty one years ago, September 9, he'd awakened in his dorm room and known that something very special was going to happen that day. And that day he'd met Grace in a psychology class.

The agnostic part of him stirred.

Now, did the feeling make me alert for something special? And thus did meeting Grace become something special to fulfill the prophecy?

Was the feeling really just from "an underdone bit of potato" in Dicken's words?

No way! Twenty-six years of true love followed that. I know that's true. That feeling was real and was a premonition, a harbinger of something that changed my life forever. And this feels just like that did.

"And it's even got special effects and life threatening situations to boot."

The sun hit the tamaracks. It shimmered through the ice encased on the branches, and made the water of the channel glimmer and flash. The cloud cover in the east went a glorious orange. Another day. Another day. And he was still here. And something, something very specific, and quite possibly very good was coming.

"What is it Huck? Any ideas?"

Huck wasn't saying, but he did look amused.

Chapter 5
Train Trip

She'd done it again. It was a kind of magic really. The little shit had talked him into, of all things, going on a cross country train trip with her, aboard the *California Zephyr*, to be at their brother's wedding in Reno.

"Face it you big doofus," she'd said, moments after she once again burst through the cabin doorway unannounced, giving him no time to remind her that he'd recently had two near death experiences and maybe needed a little more time to think about them, preferably alone, "there is no reason you shouldn't do this. What else have you got to do other than mark the progress of your toe fungus and read some poetry or some dusty old novel you've already memorized?"

"I'm a contemplative," he'd said from his old leather chair by the fire, only half kidding. As he'd said this he'd gestured with his cup of coffee and spilled enough to scald his knee, though he'd managed to breathe out, "Want some?" a moment later, so Jen wouldn't notice.

She had noticed, of course, anyway, and smirked slightly when she said, "No, I don't want any of your goddamned rancid bachelor coffee! ! I want you to give me a goddamned answer!"

"Jen, I'm going to the wedding. I'll just fly. Whirlwind trip. Why not? I mean all Jake's going to do is look at me from the altar, wink, shake my hand at the reception and say, 'Shiny' I don't need to go all Jack Kerouac for that. Day and a half I can be right back here."

"That's what I mean! You need to move! You need to grow! A week ago you damned near froze yourself, and would have if it wasn't for Huck and Tom cuddling with you, and then a day later you nearly blew them and yourself up! I wouldn't miss you much, but Huck and Tom are lovable."

"Oh nice…"

"Come on, live a little! I'll pay for the damned trip!"

Why was she so insistent about this? When had she ever wanted to go on a trip alone with him? And when had she ever paid for anything?

"Okay, wait a minute. Something's up. Something's up; I can smell it."

"Nothing's…"

"You, the cheapest skinny tight wad on the planet are going to pay for a cross country train trip for me? What's really going on here?"

Jen had turned slightly away, but not enough so he couldn't see her face, he remembered later. Then, she had started to cry.

"Oh, jesus…jesus…I'm sorry, Jen."

He'd gotten up and gone to her, wrapping his long arms around her still tiny body.

"Jen, I'm sorry. I am an irascible old coot. If you want to go across country with me on a damned one wheeled scooter I'll go. I know you're just thinking of me."

Even as he was saying those words, he was incredulous. He was going to travel across the country, by train yet, with his sister who constantly got under his skin, to see his brother, who he barely knew, get married to a trophy wife who was all of 31, in an Eastern Orthodox wedding in Reno, Nevada?

Suddenly Jen's tears had stopped and she had moved back from him holding him at arm's length. "Good. The ticket was going to go to waste if you didn't take it. Mark and I were going to go, but he got this promotion at the prison, to head up the psychology unit, so I was going to have to travel alone. He's coming out on the plane to meet us. Just a whirlwind trip, why not? There and back in a day and half. Thanks, doofus! You're such a sucker!" She'd headed for the door, opened it, exited, slammed it, then opened it again suddenly and stuck her head back in. "Oh, by the way, Jake says you're best man! There's a few responsibilities that go with that... he'll fill you in when you get there."

The door had slammed, the fire had crackled. The trap had snapped shut.

And now, here they were, in the middle of the night rambling across America, somewhere west of Chicago packed into a berth so small that even Jen had to turn sideways to get into the bathroom door. And this upper bunk. This coffin, with the ceiling three inches from his face, no window, so stuffy he had the urge to pound on the ceiling to see if somebody would dig him up. And Jen, snoring in the bunk below him! Who knew a skinny middle aged woman could snore that loud? She'd gone to sleep wondering what she would write for her column in the local newspaper, *Hunter Tales* about sleeping on a train. He had a few ideas: It's like sleeping in a camping tent going 80 miles an hour. Or it's like being a marble in a bag of marbles bouncing along in the basket of a 10-year-old boy's bike. Did bikes have baskets anymore? Other than his? The bike he'd ridden the seven miles to campus in the fall and spring for the last eight years? Was that why the kids on campus giggled when they saw him coming? Was that why some of them hummed the Wicked Witch Oz song when he passed? It didn't matter. He wanted to kill his sister. That was his focus at this moment. It wouldn't be hard, just this pillow over her face for a minute or two. Be careful not to let her kick him in the nuts while she struggled. So lovely. Then go for coffee and roll when the dining car opened. Anybody who knew her would understand.

And why the hell was he, all six foot one, 250 pounds of him in the upper bunk anyway?

"I'm claustrophobic," she'd said. "You know that, ever since you rolled me up in the hide-a-bed when I was little."

He'd like to do that again now. Hey, there was an idea. He could just grab her right now, stick her into the top bunk and fold her into the wall! Nobody would hear her. Only Mark would

miss her and he could tell Mark she'd run away with a gypsy she'd
met on the train. Or, wait, an Indian guru, or an Indian guide, or
a tour guide, or a handsome young German touring America…
Hell, he was a writer. He'd think of something. Maybe Mark would
be grateful… He'd probably take a good hunting dog in trade, no
questions asked without Ben's even bothering with a cover story…

Well, this was stupid. It was just a middle of the night thing.
He didn't really want to kill his sister…probably… What he needed
to do was go somewhere else to sleep. Or just sit in the observation
car and read. He climbed down from the top bunk as loudly as
possible. Jen didn't even stir. He contemplated emptying a bottled
water on her head. Or pouring it up her vibrating nostrils while
he held her snoring mouth shut. Then he thought better of it, as
she peacefully snored. Really, there'd just be too much paperwork
involved.

"Little sneak," he said, as he pulled on his pants and shoes,
and walked out into the narrow hall bouncing along with the train
as he went.

It was funny. All those movies he'd seen involving trains,
North by Northwest, Some Like It Hot, Silver Streak, they had it right.
It really was just like that: the bouncing around, the flashing of
lights as you passed through towns. What hit him the most as
they had passed through Chicago and other cities, even towns,
was that trains were a weird kind of time machine. They passed
through some really ugly parts of town, it was true, past garbage
heaps and industrial parks and back yards of truly poverty stricken
neighborhoods, where, he for one, would be afraid to get out.
But the weird thing was that you also passed buildings: city halls,
courthouses, hotels, power plants, mercantile, that were the most
important buildings in the city when the trains were first running.
They built them where they built them so that folks getting off the
train had easy access to the places they were going and vice versa.
These were the places where the movers and the shakers got out
to do their moving and shaking and if you, as a city planner, made
sure they didn't have to go far when they got out, the shaking and
moving might be all in your favor. And now, that was all done,

and these buildings, when not completely abandoned, were shabby shadows of the glories of the past. The trains ran on tracks through the bygone. A disappeared world with nothing left but abandoned hulks with signs now chipping away, half obscured or obliterated, marking poorly what had once been important.

As he made his way to the observation car he noticed that the spots between the cars, above the linkages, though covered, had a real feel of the outdoors coming in. That's something you never feel on a plane or in a car. Little grates beneath your feet, odd little shaking that you didn't feel elsewhere. Movement. Always movement.

He liked the concept, which trains provided, of going to sleep one place and waking up another. After so many years, so many responsibilities, he liked not being in charge. Like being a little kid falling asleep in the back of the car as he had, with Jake and Jen leaning against him. Ben remembered he had tried desperately to listen to the grown up conversations about philosophy, politics, love, and literature, that his Mom and Dad were holding in the front seat. If he could just stay awake a moment longer he'd not be so drunk on the difficulty of the words. Just stay awake until he understood… And he never did. That was the down side, but there was a big up: he'd wake up magically at home in his bed, or in the daylight in the car. Somewhere else, magic, magic.

He at last arrived at the observation car and was greeted with pitch black out the windows. They were choice seats during the day, would be especially so when they got to the Rockies he bet. Right now though there was nothing but darkness through the wrap over windows of the rounded train car. That, and the vague sense of movement as they crossed the farmland between rural towns. Not a single soul in the car with him.

He hadn't brought a book with him from the berth. Stupid, but he probably wouldn't have read anyway. He sat down and put his feet up on the window ledge. Mom would have yelled at him for that. But Mom wasn't here.

Oh don't kid yourself, chum
She's here.
Never left your gray matter.
Alone is what you want
What you'll never get.
We are always everybody we've ever known.
No need to phone.
The bones speak
in the language of spirit.
Pretend you can't hear it all you like,
Those voices will never leave.

He'd have to write that one down. He pulled his little notebook out of his pocket and began doing so. How long had he been doing this? How many notebooks? How many notebooks with poems nobody would ever see and some that a few would? Interspersed with grocery lists, ideas for writing assignments for his students, quotes he'd found in reading. Over a hundred he bet. How many a year? Over, say, 45 or so years? Going back to when he was in high school, junior high even. Many. Too many.

On the top of the page where he was writing his poem was Dale' Sylvanus's number which was probably also in 10 or twelve other notebooks. He still remembered the look on Dale's face when he brought him around the camp, down the hill to the basement window.

"Holy shit! Doctor O'Brian, you are one lucky son of a bitch! Oh sorry, sorry. I'm just glad you wasn't hurt." Dale had punctuated this by spitting a sizable chaw of tobacco into the snow of the front yard. He'd pulled down his John Deere cap and shook his head scratching behind his left ear at his close cropped red gray hair.

Ben had laughed. And for the 100th time he'd said, "Dale, you really have to call me Ben."

"That's a hard sell, Doc. A hard sell."

He'd been Ben's student back when Ben was still teaching high school. Ben was 35 and Dale was 15 then and there was just no taking the respect out of the boy even though they were now 60 and 40. That's why the cussing was so funny. So out of their usual realm, though obviously more like the real Dale than the respectful "Dr. O'Brian" part.

Dale was a Gulf War veteran, and Afghanistan too briefly, and together with about five other men of about the same age from around the area they formed what Grace used to term, "the little tribe" They looked out for each other through thick and thin. Most of them had difficult marriages or were on their second or third. They drank a good bit as well, and may have done some drugs, definitely marijuana. To Ben, that was all a big "So what?" at this point and after what they'd been through in the war, but the long and the short of it was that whatever job they were doing for you might not be their main priority at any given time. Ben had always been okay with that, though it was irritating as hell at times. Grace had been able to get them to hop to it more, but Ben was a softer touch, and now that she was long gone, jobs got done much more slowly. Ben didn't really care. Not at all really. Dale and his friends knew that too. Still, when things like this happened, they rallied around Ben. Those fellows were worker bees on this project, and had Ben's window repaired, the old furnace out and the new propane furnace in in just a few days. The new furnace ran great. Kept the place way warmer than it had been in years. And all in record time for Dale and his pals. Truth was, Ben liked those guys very much. And, truth be told, he liked himself better because he employed them. Dale's surname was Sylvanus, which had always puzzled Ben, since Dale claimed Irish ancestry. Once the subject had come up out at camp with Dale and his father. John, the father, had told Ben that the family legend was that when John's grandfather had gotten to Ellis Island, he'd been met there by a Greek customs agent who took one look at the name O'Sylvan and had told the ancestor that he wasn't spelling his name right. "Any good Greek," the family quote went, "would know the name is "Sylvanus". Thus, the name. John said his grandfather had contemplated changing it to Woods, but there were several Woods families already in the area, so they'd left it at "Sylvanus" and left people to wonder why there was so much red hair in the family. And there was! Dale, his father, Dale's daughter, Kelly and his son Donnie as well. 'What's in a name', was never truer, Ben thought.

"Next time, Doc, you might want to have me check things out before you fire the furnace up." Dale had said after further inspecting the furnace that first day. Then he'd grinned, a tooth or two missing from his lower jaw. Three days later after they'd finished the work while Ben had been away in town, he'd gone down to inspect the work. On the new furnace he'd found the following note:

BOYS AND ME GLAD YOUR OKAY. ALL WORK DONE. BILL YOU LATER OR STOP BY AT GARAGE WHEN GET CHANC. PLEASE DON'T MESS WITH FURNACE **AT ALL** (last two words underlined four times). IF ANYTHING WRONG COME AND GET ME. DONT WANT YOU BLOWED UP DOC.
DALE

Later, Ben knew, Dale and his pals would have a tale to tell to their buddies in the bar about ol' Doc O'Brian and the other pencil pushers from the college. Still, Ben believed Dale genuinely liked him. And he was right.

A few days after the blow up and repair, Dale had stopped in at Ray Antilla's sugar shack along the Gros Rocher River north of Hunter. The river was known locally as "The Gross Roach" or " The Grossy." Ben had always thought it would be easier just to call the water the Big Rock or the Rock, since the Voyageur who had named it was no doubt referring to the enormous glacial boulder along a bend a mile north of Ray's camp. But, as Ben well knew, fighting local custom, especially when it came to language, was a losing battle.

Dale had stopped by at Ray's sugar shack that day because he was helping out Ray, too. Consciously or unconsciously, with both their cars and their homes, Dale was involved in an effort at trying to keep the faculty from wiping itself out. Dale's current concern, in the form of Ben's furnace and Ray's sap boiling wood

stove, was faulty heating systems. Ray Antilla was a math professor
at the college who, like Ben, had grown up locally. The shack was
a fixture by this time and a hangout for professors, high school
teachers, and a couple of local business men. The place was a
monstrosity. Ray, who had a sense of humor not unlike Ben's, liked
it that way.

It had started as just a sugar shack in the Antilla family's
maple stand above The Grossy. Ray liked the idea of building the
shack on those fine 40 acres and loved the idea of making the syrup
having no idea at all of how to go about doing either. He'd slugged
ahead anyway, with Dale and the boys helping him out, and Ben
lending a hand with Jen's husband Mark. Mark was useful that way:
he actually knew what he was doing with saws and hammers. He
even used power tools. Ben, frankly, knew even less than Ray about
building and way less about syrup making.

The shack had started as just one room for the stove, under
a little peaked roof, with a couple cast off chairs and a ratty old
couch inside . There was a leanto, at first, on the uphill side and a
door, which was a castoff from the local high school where Ben had
been teaching at the time, bolted into an uninsulated wood frame
structure.

The first addition after that was the bunk beds built by
Mark on the wall furthest from the stove, to avoid the steam rising
from the sap. Dale had rigged up an ingenious spring-loaded trap
door in the roof to allow the sweet steam to escape. Cute little
structure to start. Then Ray got an idea. It would be a great place to
deer hunt too, and the Grossy was terrific duck hunting this close
to Lake Superior, especially on rough days on the big lake. Why
not build on another room? So they did, a full on bunk house on
the uphill side, complete with peekaboo pictures which slid aside
so the guys could shoot at passing deer and a duck blind, which
though not connected, was built, just forty steps down hill.

What, though, was a hunting camp without a dining room?
So that addition too was made. Soon, Camp Grossy was loaded
down with eager sappers and pseudo-sappers, hunters and pseudo-
hunters and more room was needed. Rooms kept appearing.

Some with windows in walls facing into interior rooms, multiple doors leading to ridiculous destinations, ladders, lofts, porches, and verandas. By the time of the latest sugar shack symposium at Camp Grossy the place had three floors, multiple wings, and a platform high up among the maple branches with no safety railings of any kind, known as "Fear and Trembling Post". The deal was, all newcomers had to go up and stand there on the narrow platform high in the treetops in the sometimes brisk wind coming off the Grossy, and chug a beer. If they did so, they got to write their names and a message on the underside of the platform while standing on the not, so secure ladder beneath it. More than one Camp Grossy initiate had awakened the morning after his initiation clinging to his bunk in a nightmare of cold sweat at the memory of his initiation of the night before.

Ray, who was a quiet gentle sort with a dry sense of humor and penchant for speaking only to deliver a one liner at exactly the right moment, had a way of tipping his head back, taking a little gasp of air, then letting out a chuckle of pure enjoyment, which was Ben's favorite thing about him.

It was Ray who had named the subject of that day's symposium: Ben's trip with his sister to Reno aboard a train. Ben was already regretting having mentioned the subject. Also present, at the "symposium" were Ray's sister Bev, a small tough old girl of about 70 who could arm wrestle any of them and had been the home-ec teacher at Hunter High for 40 years; Mark, and Matt Esposito, who had arrived at the college from Boston on an English fellowship about the time Ben came aboard, and who was known as "Mutt" for several reasons including his perpetually uncombed hair and penchant for drooling and slurping between long-winded sentences.

"Sorry I brought it up," Ben had said, of the train trip, as hilarity ensued.

"I'm glad I got the promotion at the prison," Mark said, "but the idea that you and Jen will be together all the way to Reno in a closed room almost makes me wish I could bug the place."

"What's your take, Ray?," Mutt said, after a long swig from

a dark home brewed beer, "think the two of 'em will survive the trip? O.B. is not near so tolerant as Hicks. And Jen, well, she's skinny, but she's mighty!"

"You guys," Bev said, "could benefit from listening to Jen once in a while. She talks good sense."

"Absolutely," Mark added quickly, which resulted in a whoop of condemnation from Mutt, and a classic Ray gasp and laugh.

"Ah, is that the moon I see, Petruchio?" Mutt grinned, slurped and laughed.

"Did I ever deny I'm not in charge? Hey, I've seen the boss's job. I don't want it."

" Really though (slurp) can you imagine the dialogue?" Mutt added, focusing back on the Ben and Jen train trip, followed by a long slurp. "They *will* kill each other!"

"And what kind of romance can O.B. get going with his little sister looking on?" Ray added, extending his usual needle.

"Hell, it'd be no different from the way it started with Grace," Mark said.

"Shut up, Mark! God, why do I tell you anything?" Ben said.

Jen's voyeur view of Ben and Grace's first amorous flight, really wasn't a secret to anybody else, but the pretense was part of the fun.

"Yup, they were out there skinny dipping and what not and Jen's sitting there on the beach finding out about the birds and the bees!'"

"Easy you boys," Bev said, sobering up the room. "This is Gracie we're talking about. You can rip on Ben all you like, but as long as I'm here, Grace is off limits.

Grace. It always came back to her, from their first night together at the lake, to that summer ten years ago, five years after her passing, when he slept on the beach and talked to her, and half believed she was there with him, to this very moment on the train. The memory of that first night at the lake sometimes helped to smooth out the darkness. He had been 19 and he'd brought her from campus on a trip through the Seney Wildlife Refuge and then out to camp. They'd sat together with Jen and Mom at the beach fire until the latter two had supposedly gone to bed, except Jen hadn't. Then, one thing had led to another. He could still feel Grace's sexy smooth wet skin, see the freckles on her chest in the moonlight, hear their voices as they came together out in the still water, then hear his mother's voice call out for Jen, and then dimly see Mom see their clothes on the beach.

"We're fine, Mom," he'd called out in a voice that broke, and Grace had giggled, and then there was a quick scuffling sound and Mom and Jen had disappeared. God, it had been so lovely.

How many times on the beach ten years ago, had he gone over and over that night in his head, trying desperately to use that sweet memory to block out the horrors of the hospital; the cold sadness of the funeral and the months even years of Mike's mad depression?

He'd tried and failed on that beach, ten summers ago, to block out the still sadder memory of Kate who never said a word about her mom until six days before her wedding. She had walked in through the camp doorway and looked him right in the eye.

"What would Mom think?"

"Of what?"

"Of David."

"Well, I think Dave's just fine."

"Dad, I know what 'just fine' means, and I know you think he's not good enough for me, don't even try denying it. That's not what I want to know. What would Mom think?"

"She'd love him. She'd smile at him and tell me she thought he was cute and just what you needed."

She'd cocked her head at that point, and said, "Really?"

He'd nodded, and then she had come all unglued, a look of pure hopeless doubt he'd never seen before on her face and she'd stayed with him for two days, just crying it all out. David had called and he'd told him it would be all right, though he wasn't sure that was true. Mark had come over and talked to her. The killer was that Kate needed her mom more than ever right then, not just as a mom, but also as a psychiatrist. And Grace was only in the wind.

And now all these memories
Out the dark train window
Rolling, clattering across a continent
with my muddled brain that holds them.
Wellsprings of my life:
My sister
My daughter
My brother
My son
My friends
My long gone wife
My life, sparking thoughts across the wide stretches of my soul
Reflected in the dark window
Campfires on the rolling landscape.

"Whatcha writing?"

"Grace?"

But it wasn't Grace. Not quite. He'd been so startled, sitting there in this alien place, when the woman had said those words. He'd felt like he'd been dreaming. He may have been. But the writing was in front of him in the notebook. Had he actually said his wife's name out loud?

"I'm…I'm sorry. What did you ask me?"

"Didn't mean to intrude. Sorry if I startled you."

She stood before him, a woman in her late 40's he guessed: slim, dark graying hair, dark complexion, athletic, a backpack slung over her shoulder. She had apparently just walked in.

"No, no, it's fine. Please, sit down."

She did, on the seat nearest him.

"I was feeling a little lonely," she said, almost to herself, "and you looked friendly. Sorry if I'm…oh I've interrupted…something I'm….silly." She looked about her seemingly as confused as he, then said absently, "My stop is coming up."

Jesus, she sounds exactly like Grace. And the tilt of her head, the gray strands in her dark hair...

"What? Your stop? Out here? It's so dark."

She laughed. There was a sexy lilt to it.

Just like Grace...Oh God, oh my God, God, what are you doing to me? This is the thing isn't it? The thing I felt was coming...

"It will get lighter in the morning?" she smiled.

He was done for, absolutely done for. What the hell was happening?

"Yeah, yeah, sure. Where are we anyway?"

"Coming up on Harbinger, Iowa in about a half hour. I'll be the only one getting off."

Seriously? The name of the town is 'Harbinger'.

"Um...How do you know you'll be the only one getting off?"

She laughed again and a trill of pure delight worked in his head and heart.

"Small town," she said smiling. "And I'm the only travel agent."

"Oh yeah...I know the feeling. Ben O'Brian from Hunter, Michigan."

"Never heard of it."

"Of course not."

She smiled. "Small town?"

"Probably smaller than Harbinger?"

He couldn't believe this was happening. The name of the town was Harbinger. It even had a sappy sad ending built in. Love on a train, strangers in the god forsaken cornfed night of the North American continent, they fall in love, but then her stop comes up.

"Come on..." Oh jesus, he'd said that out loud.

"Where are we going?" That smile again.

"Oh...I'm so sorry. I guess I'm sleepy or just old. Stuff is coming out that's meant to stay in."

"Like the scarecrow?"

"Ha...if I only had a brain."

Despite his best efforts, this was going well.

"Where are you headed?"

"To Reno. My brother's wedding. Old bachelor, finally succumbing."

"Funny, I've heard it's usually anything other than marriage that old men succumb to."

"Ah...cynicism in the corn belt. So refreshing."

She laughed again. "And you? Are you alone?"

"Yes, well no..."

"Ha, don't like the sound of that."

"I'm alone in the sense that I'm not married...I was...wife died 15 years ago. But I'm traveling with my little sister."

"Is she 7 or very short?"

"What? No." He laughed, in pure amazement, delight. "Force of habit. She's ten years younger, always been a tag-a-long, always in my business. She...even this train trip... Well, she's my little sister."

"I have two daughters, and I have five sisters and a brother. I know the type. So...your Grace has been gone fifteen years?"

He thought he was dreaming for a moment, then realized. "Oh, that was out loud too?"

She nodded.

"Yes. Fifteen years." He looked out into the dark.

"You...you really loved her." Ben looked over at her, at a loss.

She blushed, sputtered in a very un-Grace like way he thought, which came as a bit of a relief. " Ah, what am I doing?" she said. "I'm sorry. I hardly know what I'm saying. Just woke up. Really none of my business."

Ben, also at a loss, felt something else slip. "You sound like her..." oh god.

"Really?"

"Yes...you even look a little like...I'm sorry."

"Why?"

"I don't know, I feel like I should be. Old Catholic habit."

"Don't old nuns wear those?" She smiled.

He laughed. It was just the kind of joke he and Grace...

"You're funny."

"And I sound like your wife. Why should either of us feel odd about that? We both do though. Don't we?"

He nodded.

"You know what? What *is*...well...it just is. What we feel is real, at least at this moment. We're both too old to pretend it isn't."

"Well, I guess *I* am," he said. What she'd said about feeling something real, he could hear Grace saying, "Feel it real, Ben. Take in what is. Live right now." Oh...god.

"My name is Valerie."

"From Harbinger, Iowa."

"Uh, huh."

"It's very nice to meet you, Valerie."

He put out his hand. She did too. They laughed then realized they were still clasping each other's hands in something that was not a handshake. He gently pulled his hand back.

"How long were you and Grace married?"

"21 years. We met in college when we were 19. She was a psychiatrist."

That smile again. "At 19?"

"Ha! No, by the time she was a head-shrinker she was 30 or so. I wasn't a PhD until 35. She told me when I was done, that I could get my next degree with my next wife."

"A teacher? Professor?"

"English, yes."

"And a poet."

" Well. Yes."

"Published?"

"Actually, quite a bit."

"Well..." She laughed raising an eyebrow.

"I'm trying to impress you."

"I noticed. Not much point. My stop's coming up."

"Does it stop there?"

She looked at him for moment. Her eyes were deep blue. A definite difference. Grace's were green. Then she smiled. "Oh, you are a poet."

"Valerie what?"

"Careful."

"Oh, I probably sound like a stalker."

"Hey I interrupted you, remember? No I mean, careful, you hardly know me. Sure you want to know me better?"

"Pretty sure, yeah. Why, are you dangerous?"

"My ex thought so, sometimes, but that's another story."

"We've got time."

"Not much."

"Enough?"

"Maybe."

"Then, hey, say what you want, don't what you don't."

"Okay, my ex and I had a travel agency in Harbinger, sending farmers to the Bahamas, Cancun, even Fiji, or wherever. We raised two daughters. One is in Chicago, just visited her. Another lives in Hawaii, lucky her."

"So…"

"So, my ex, William…always wanted to be called William…"

"Lot of that going around."

"What?"

"Nothing, my son, insists on *Michael* not Mike."

"Just the one child?"

"Nope, daughter too…"

"How old were they when…"

" 15 and 13."

"Oh. Must have been terrible…"

"It…was…but William."

"Long story short, he took up with our secretary. Silly, tawdry small town stuff."

"And you'd had enough and you did something that scared him."

"How do you know I did something that…"

"Remember? 'dangerous'…"

The laugh again. " Oh yeah…well…I caught them and I fired a little metal globe that sat on my desk right at his head. Bullseye"

"You were at work and you caught them…"

"In medias res…"

"Coitus interruptus…"

She sighed, laughed again. "Exactly. I knocked him cold. Then the secretary and I had to take him to the emergency room. That was a lovely ride."

He burst out laughing. "Oh…oh god." He shook his head.

She smiled. "Sorry…didn't mean to laugh…

"Well, it's funny isn't it?"

She was so charming. He nodded. "How long ago?"

"11 years. Girls were just little. We hung together for a little while. Even fired the secretary, but he went back to her. By then I was calm. I just took the business. He moved to Chicago with her. Get bulletins from my daughters. That's about it."

"Tough."

"Not as tough as yours."

"Hard to say."

They were quiet for a long time looking out at the lightening landscape. He could make out the grain elevators on the horizon. And it suddenly occurred to him.

"Your stop coming up?"

"Uh huh."

"Listen, I…"

"We better not. This was nice. Let's keep it simple. You're going to Reno. I'm going back to Harbinger. Then you're going back to Michigan. I've got family in Iowa, and you in Detroit or wherever…"

"Ha, far from Detroit! Upper Michigan, on Lake Superior."

"Oh, way up there!"

"Ya, you betcha!"

"Like Fargo?"

"Like da U.P."

"Sounds rustic."

"So does Harbinger."

"It is. Lots of farms."

"I can see that."

There was silence again. The train began to slow.

"Can I…"

She shook her head. "Please, just stay here…but…" She sighed, smiled at him. Stood up. Then, hesitating for a moment, leaned down, set down her backpack and kissed him hard and then softly, delicately. It lasted. Their lips parted with the slightest little sound."

"Valerie from Harbinger, Iowa."

"Do you want to remember?"

"I do."

"Then remember." She kissed him again. Waved, pulled up her backpack and without looking back quickly exited the car.

He sat stunned. The train stopped. Then, with his mind wandering wildly, the train was suddenly moving again, in the dawn light he could just make out the tiny train stop and he saw a figure going to a car in the small parking lot. The figure stopped and turned toward the train in the half light of dawn.

"Valerie from Harbinger, Iowa…oh. Oh Jesus. What's her last name?"

Chapter 6
Val

What in the world have I done? The poor man. He's alone on a train in the middle of the night in a place he doesn't know and I've accosted him! If I were a man it would have been sexual assault! Well, maybe not. It was just a kiss. Barely a peck on the beak really. Oh, who am I kidding, that was a great kiss! He seemed to enjoy it. I know I did. But, it was just a kiss. Beautiful really. Sweet.

Oh god. What will the girls think? Susan will be shocked. She gets shocked so easily at anything I do that's vaguely…human. Marcy will think it's funny. People from Hawaii think everything is funny. They have that luxury. And William…well the hell with him. I hope he finds out soon.

Will I ever stop being angry with him? If not by now, maybe never.

It was just a moment. Move on girl. Just a lovely little moment. One to treasure. Let it go.

Ben O'Brian, college professor, English was it…sure…he's a poet. "Published quite often" wasn't it? He was cute with that. It would be good to date somebody literate for once. I wonder if I said anything ungrammatical. Well, that kiss was ungrammatical. I love to talk about books. When have I dated anybody who could talk about books? I wonder what he thinks of Willa Cather. I love My Antonia. Or Jane Smiley. He's a poet…Emily Dickinson then, Sharon Olds, Anne Sexton, for that matter, Whitman, Cummings, Sandburg, Frost, Pablo Neruda or maybe the

Romantics? Shakespeare. I bet he loves Shakespeare. "Shall I compare thee to a summer's day..." Oh...what am I thinking?

I didn't give him my last name. Sort of on purpose. I mean, he could be a real creep.

No. No, he isn't. He was genuinely surprised by the whole thing. Gracious. A little disarming with that wit. He just seemed very nice: compassionate. He was genuinely interested and amused by what I had to say. He didn't have time to prepare a line of crap to impress me. Still, he could be trouble for me. It wouldn't be that hard to find me even without my last name.

And what if he did? Wouldn't that be a good thing? He didn't look the computer type though. What if he can't find me? That might be much worse. Oh face it girl, you really want to see him again. Yeah... what if he can't find me? Val, you fool, why didn't you just give him your information? What if he can't find me? Ha, sounds like if he tells his sister, she will. What would that be like, I wonder? Third degree I'm betting. She sounds like a peach. Oh, Val, you don't even know her. She's probably quite sweet. All older brothers resent their little sisters, even if they are in their 50's.

It wouldn't be that hard to find him.

Oh. come on. It's impossible. Two old farts had a nice moment. That's it. Back to Harbinger, Iowa. A trip to Fiji later this year. Certainly not to the Upper Peninsula of Michigan. Sounds cold. Really cold. Lots of snow. Way more than we get. The people are probably alike though. Rural, into everybody's business, or focused solely on their own in some log cabin. Is this really happening? Am I really thinking these things? Why did I kiss him? I need to get back to reality. Back to my life.

When I get to the office I'll Google him. Should I? Yes.

Valerie Traeger pulled the Forerunner out of the little parking lot of what passed for a train station in Harbinger, Iowa and headed up the street towards what passed for downtown. She turned right at one of three traffic lights, right next to the Old World Cafe where her sister Bunny and Bunny's daughter Cindy worked. Then she headed east towards the travel agency.

That was a nice kiss. Oh stop it. You had a moment. You had a nice moment. Get back to work. Been gone a week, probably tons in backlog. Timmy is pretty good for an intern. And the price is right. Good to have family. Better get something to eat. I'll call Bunny, have her bring over some fresh oatmeal and the homemade rye toast. Something for Timmy too. He likes the muffins. Oh splurge, you've met a nice guy. How about some granola, maybe even some eggs!

For heaven's sakes, what do you need with a man after all this time? He seemed nice though. He was almost like a little boy the way he sat there. Oh, that didn't sound good. But that's not how it was. Seemed like a nice man. A little lost, pretty soulful…well…he's a poet. And he's published. I bet I could order one of his books. Wouldn't that be something? Look right into his psyche. That's a little creepy. But what an opportunity!

Do I want to know that much before we even start? All I'd be doing is reading his work, showing an interest. And he has a job or had one. Okay, he has a pension. It's not about the money. Not at all, but to know he's secure that way…to know for certain that he won't be asking me to float him a loan. Oh, you met the man; that's not a guy who would do that even if he was desperate. He really seemed honest, just good. A little older. Stop it, stop it!

She pulled into the parking lot of Small World Travel, formerly Hofsteder's Travel. The sun was just coming up. She sighed at the thought of the backlog on her desk.

It's always a pain to get started again. It makes me wish Grandpa Traeger had never given me that atlas when I was a little girl. That's what started all this. Careful what you give your grandkids for Christmas! Just the thought of the messages piled up makes me wish I'd never left. My life has become nothing but work. You have to make money. How much money do you have to make? Enough to retire. Enough to have something to draw on. Something to share? With a man maybe? A certain man?

Oh, stop it. Stop it. Looks like a nice day. Maybe I'll go for a walk by the river after my desk clears…next Thursday. What if there isn't a backlog? What if when I left everybody just assumed we were closing for good? What if nobody from Harbinger ever wants to travel anywhere again? What if they all just start booking their own flights and cruises on the internet. Ha, most of them don't have the internet. Most of them have a hard time with the TV remote. Thank God for that, or I'd be out of work. Oh come on. Come on. You love your customers. You do right by them. You

*custom design their trips based on what you know about them. And in this
little town you can't help knowing everything about them. You make it all
a small world for them. Safe, happy, yet still an adventure. Nice sales pitch.
Are you buying it? Sure, why not? It's worked so far.*

    *The sign is fading a little. Better get that touched up. Maybe have
Timmy do it. He's a bit of an artist. Oh, I just want him to follow the lines.
Just keep that as it is. Then again, he might want to do something new. Oh
let him. New look. New look.*

    *This wouldn't have anything to do with the man on the train
would it? Ben. Benjamin must be. Ben O'Brian from Hunter, Michigan.
He is handsome. And smart, and funny. What are you looking for in a
man? Handsome, smart, and funny is a pretty good start. The pension
makes him solid. And those poems just waiting to be read might fill in
any other details. I wonder if he's got a blog. No. No I'm pretty sure not.
Twentieth century man written all over him. He lives in the sticks. Then,
again, so do I. Who am I to judge? There can't be that much difference
between Hunter and Harbinger.*

    *I wonder if he hunts. Probably fishes too. That's a way of life there.
Like it is here for a lot of men. But most guys who hunt and fish don't write
poetry. Most guys who write poetry don't live in Harbinger or Hunter. He's
atypical. So are you. You've always felt out of synch with this town. Always
felt just a little too good for it. Always felt guilty about that feeling too. You
always cover fast if you say something around your sisters that hints that
way. They still think I'm that way, though. Miss stuck up. I bet lots of folks
think that about him too. Too good for Hunter, one of the college crowd. Still,
he seems like a regular guy. Probably gets along with the guys at hunting
camp and the hardware store just fine. Look, he is who he is. So are you.
Nobody should ever feel guilty about that.*

    *He's had kids and they're out in the world. He's been through
the wars. And losing his wife. That's tough. That's tough. You could see that
pain still in his eyes when he mentioned her. If you get the book, be ready
to read about her. She'll be in there big time. She's in him big time, but why
not? Of course she is. She would be. The things that happen in our lives
create us when they don't destroy us. Did I read that somewhere? Maybe I
made it up. Maybe I'm a poet. Ha, no way.*

    Whatever Ben O'Brian is, he's a man and he's flawed just like you are. He looks like he does the best he can and isn't always happy with the results. He's pretty humble, and seems to like his life for the most part. He's doing well. You're doing well. Why in the hell shouldn't the two of you do well together?

Face it old girl, you're going to Google him.

Chapter 7
Investigation

Really now. Ben met a woman, who just happens to sound almost exactly like and look somewhat like Grace. On a train, in the middle of the night. And…they kissed. Then she disappeared to a place called "Harbinger, Iowa" Really, 'Harbinger', really. No symbolism there. You don't have to be Fellini to figure that one out! God. He's gone again. I can't take him any place nice. We sat there in the observation car going over the continental divide today. Absolutely gorgeous. There was a golf course in a tiny town up there with guys walking around carrying clubs and fly rods in their golf bags. And Ben didn't even comment on that. He didn't even stare, like he usually does at the natural beauty: jagged peaks, mountain meadows, huge expanses of "holy crap" height and space, skies so blue it hurt your eyes. All he could talk about was this imaginary woman and their imaginary kiss. Ben was in euphoria, incredibly happy. When is he ever in euphoria? When is he ever even visibly happy? Normally, when he's grumpy I figure that's as close as he's going to get to happy and I settle for that. And he was mostly silent! Really? I mean, when does he not expound? He always expounds! "This world is going to hell in a hand basket!" "Oh brave new world that hath such people in't" "There is nothing either good or bad but thinking makes it so" "Not with a bang but a whimper" none of that usual crap.

I MEAN, JUST THINK ABOUT THIS: HE TOLD ME

ABOUT THE WOMAN WITHOUT MY EVEN HAVING TO ASK!!!

Ben O'Brian who guards his and other people's privacy so closely that he won't even gossip, not ever not even a little bit. Oh he's gone again.

I think the old doofus is really in love. Trouble is, I think it's with a figment of his imagination. Oh…I'm scared for him. It's a little like that time when he turned 50. We couldn't get him in off the beach. He was out there talking to himself. Sometimes it was like he was talking to Grace. He'd say something and then pause like he was listening. So terrifying. And Mike says he was on the verge of offing himself with his buck knife on that last night. He got better after that, though. Couldn't get much out of Mike, just like his dad that way, but it had something to do with that story he always told about Mike catching an eagle feather in the sunrise or some such shit. It really is hard to get anything out of the men in this family. Except for Jake. He and I have always been open books to each other. Funny, he hardly speaks to Ben. It makes me die laughing when he gives Ben that "Shiny" shit. The look on Ben's face: priceless. He thinks Ben is a lunatic too. And he loves to see the old doofus get worked up. But Mike? There's a hard nut to crack. Even harder than getting something out of the doofus. That's what bothers me about him and his imaginary girlfriend: Ben just out and out told me this! He seemed to take pleasure in telling me!

I told him I was going to Google her.

He said, "Goog away!" Then he laughed like a moron until all the folks in the observation car started staring. I told him we should go back to the berth and talk this out. He didn't even argue. So we went back to the berth and just sat there on a gorgeous sunny day watching the Colorado River and the Rockies go by and he just kept telling me the same thing over and over. All about this woman who disappeared in this tiny town in the darkness. Claims the train stopped. I didn't remember stopping. That's when he really pissed me off. He grinned that horse's ass grin of his and said I was snoring so loud when he came back after kissing the glorious Valerie, that "the sound of your snores and the tremors they caused in your canary bones probably kept you from feeling the stoppage." So I checked with the porter and damned if we hadn't stopped in Harbinger, Iowa of all places. So, the place at least, is not a delusion. Later he got up, said he was going to set up dinner for us in the dining car, his treat! Big joke, it's all included and I'm buying. Wouldn't mind so much, even paying for the doofus's dinner, but this being forthcoming of his is driving me nuts! It's like playing tennis with the net down. I don't trust that I'm getting the true score.

So I Googled her. Harbinger, Iowa, travel agencies. Well, Harbinger's only got about 3,000 people in the town proper. Lots of farms around, adding maybe another 1,000 so naturally there's only one travel agency. Amazing there's even one really, but lots of people want to get out of Iowa, I suppose, and they're old so, just like in Hunter, they can't figure out the internet. That baffles me, really. I'm not so young anymore and I can't figure out what's so hard, or why Ben gets so worked up about it. Made him get an iPhone. Can't get him to text, though. He barely e-mails. Doesn't answer the phone if I call him, so I have to go out to that damned camp. He's still got the house in Hunter, but he's been threatening to sell it "to some big time real estate tycoons who have offered top dollar". He always says that with his doofus grin which tells me he's trying to get me to investigate and find out it's his friend Mutt who's expressed an interest or some such. Anyway, he's threatening to insulate the camp so he can live out there all winter. I tell him it's a summer place. Always was. He tells me it's a camp. Always was. Guess it's a matter of whether you asked Mom or Dad and now they're both gone and Jake isn't interested, so it's up to the two of us and we just go back and forth. And he smiles at me. Smiles at me and says, "It's a camp, sneak. Always was, Dad and I were always just humoring you and Mom by letting you come out in the summer." And that cocky smile of his is so sickening anyway. Just makes me want to punch him. And now he's smiling all the time. Makes me sick.

Nobody is going to know who he is at the wedding! "Who's the guy that looks like Ben who's smiling?" They'll ask.

"Well, that used to be Ben," I'll say, "but now he's haunted by a living ghost." That's right, I said *living* because damned if I didn't find her! "Valerie Traeger, proprietor of *Small World Travel*, she's 48. She's got two daughters, Susan, 24, a systems analyst in Chicago, and Marcy, 22, student at U of Hawaii, intern at an art gallery. Valerie, is divorced, just like Ben said, 11 years ago, from William Hofsteader 50, now of Champagne, Illinois, remarried to Carolyn Collins, now divorced, re-remarried to Tiffany (of course) Hawkins, 27. Bet she's blonde and has big tits. Oh, here's a picture of her in a bikini, next to the daughter who looks none too happy about it. Yup, big ones. What a cliche. Hope they're all suing him for everything.

Jesus, *I'm* starting to like the mystery woman. Ben says Valerie got the agency and that's all she wanted. She sounds nice, like Ben said. And she's not flashy looking. Kind of *Mother Earth News* type. Backpacks, hiking sandals. She's done the John Muir Trail. No small feat I hear. She's kind of cute really. But she's not Grace. Grace was gorgeous. An exotic beauty, everybody said so. We were like sisters. She kind of got a kick out of me and the way I teased Ben, I think. Ah, face it. I idolized her… Oh Gracie, what has your man gone and done?

Anyway, I'm not going to fall for her nice appearance, and her hard luck story about her asshole husband or any of that other shit! What the hell is this Iowa woman doing kissing my brother on a train in the middle of the night? She doesn't even know him. He might be a serial killer. I worry for her.

No…damnit! I should be worrying for the doofus. Maybe she's a serial kisser. Maybe she does this all the time. There's no string of attachments on her Facebook, though. Then, I guess there wouldn't be if she was blackmailing them or something. She says here, "blissfully unattached". Sounds like something Ben would write if he had ever considered Facebook. I remember I mentioned it to him once and he damned near threw me out of the camp, like that time I put him on the dating website without telling him. He came right over to the house and absolutely forbade me from "meddling in his affairs" ever again. Even Mark glared at me when I started laughing at the use of the word "affairs". Guess maybe I overstepped that time.

Oh, who am I kidding? Ben is a catch. He's good looking, smart, honest, loyal to a ridiculous point, and just a good man. In two minutes any woman would know he was harmless. Nicest guy on the planet, except to me. Nasty old curmudgeon. Except for now. He couldn't be more pleasant! I hate him so much!

Well, this is impossible. I mean, how can I get him to understand that he and this Valerie just had a moment? That's all it was. It's nice for them both, but what could possibly come of it? She comes from a family of six with about a million relatives right in that area. Granted she's a travel agent, but she's got oak roots in that community. And Ben couldn't be more sedentary if he was granite. Wouldn't you know it, I get him out of that camp for a week and he finds love. And he'll never thank me. He'll never thank me. Except he might. The mood he's in. He's liable to walk right into this little room and plant a big wet kiss on my cheek and thank me for bringing him on this train trip. I swear if I could get out of this train I'd jump off one of these mountains! Damn him for confounding all of my expectations. He's become so hard to keep track of! That never used to be a problem. "What's Ben up to?" people would ask and I'd just raise an eyebrow and say, "At camp reading and writing, where else?" Just when I think I've got him all figured out he hands me a poem, that makes me cry like that one he wrote about me years ago.

My sister, the moon over the water,
Watches me rise early to hunt and fish and paddle.
She catalogues my foibles,
Arbitrates my inward squabbles,
Hears me mumbling and humming in the boat
In the crystalline dark.

She shines out clear over calm, cold waters.
Plays hide and seek when the clouds come,
Coy, flighty girl.
She is married to the dawn

Who speaks in his time
In his wide, red voice across the horizon

She is a good wife to him,
Seeking always his best interest in her darkness.
Taunting and teasing his grandeur
Just before he shines

She humbles men
Reminds them with her wisps of mystery
Of the reason for their darker longings.

She is the haunting light.
She makes the shining path
Which all men wish to follow,
On still nights.

She leads the way through the dark.
Wickedly wonders aloud in a voice of light
Just what we men would do with the ebony delights.
She hides, just beyond the black.
And having silently said just enough,
Leads us back to day and all
That must be done.

Seriously, how big a doofus do you have to be to write something that nice about somebody and still have them want to spit in your smug writer/professor eyes and smack that dumbass smile off your now-I'm-in-love-and-I'm-60-nyah-nyah-nyah face? I hate him. I love him. He's my brother. What can I say?

He's telling me the truth, at least as far as he knows it about this woman. What am I gonna do? Why would this woman want that old doofus? Does she want him? Damnit, if she's kissing him full on the mouth on a fucking train in the middle of the night in the middle of America, she better want him! If she breaks his heart I'll hunt her down and kill her with Dad's old Ithaca pump that

Mark keeps in the closet. Don't think I won't.

So, a couple of minutes ago, he walks in and hands me this poem that he's written about Valerie and says, "It's deeply personal. Please don't share it with anyone, but I wanted you to see, if I look her up, that I'm not taking this lightly and this is important to me. And if, in a couple of days, it all fades away…" and for the first time in a couple of days his face looked a little pained when he said that "…just burn it, and please don't tell anybody."

Do you know what that is? That's trust, he's trusting me! I want to cry. Anyway, here's the damned poem, screw him, I've got to share it with somebody:

For Valerie

I'll always remember now
That my heart's fire needs tending.
That the wind in the hemlocks is talking.
That the brave morning needs my courage too.
We're all in love with each other:
Birch trees and elk grass,
Muskrat and great blue heron,
The old log camp and the lake water,
Stars and comets,
And, yes,
Man and woman on a train across the plains.

We only lose track of this fact
When those dimwit human voices:
Surrounding walls of chattering chaos,
Crumble down like bank erosion
Over our souls and anxious eyes
And drown us in the flood of doubt
That too often carries love away.

"So, go to the grate," I'll say to myself
From now to always

If ever that heart fire dims again.
"Do your damnedest
In whatever god awful awkward way you can."

"Never mind the burns,
just tend your fire."

Ah doofus, what have you got yourself into now?

Chapter 8
A Trail Map
(Partly Existential, Partly Transcendental)
of Ben O'Brian's route to his current predicament
in Yosemite's Mariposa Grove and His Forthcoming
Intrepid Rescue by His Holy Fool Son

Part I: The Predicament

March 18, 2016

Well, this is a fucking disaster. I couldn't just kill myself back at the camp by blowing myself up or walking off into a blizzard, I had to travel by train to my brother's bizarro Ukrainian wedding in Reno of all places, then let my holy fool of a son, who may be dead by now since I left him with a concussion back in the camper at the south entrance of the Mariposa Grove Trails, great parent, and then headed off leaving my compass in my bag in the camper without checking the weather forecast, which probably said, "… locally heavy snow squalls, and by the way don't fucking go into the Mariposa Grove on skis without a compass you fucking idiot!" And, of course, I left the water too because I wasn't going to need it, "…only be gone a little while, heh, heh, and come back when Mike is feeling better", but then, typical me, got all mystical about the great big fucking trees and started following them into the great big fucking woods, because I just knew there'd be an even bigger even more mystical tree somewhere out there, like a kid chasing his red balloon at the fair who gets lost from his fucking idiot parents who should have been watching him. Yeah, swell morning.

Did I mention that I lost my way somewhere in the upper grove, which is complete with absolutely breathtaking mammoth trees that have been here forever and ever and I hate to quibble, since my life to them is not much, their having been here for thousands of years and all, but it's pretty important to me and I don't have any matches, and I think I may be headed the right way, but I'm not sure because the snow is coming right into my eyes!

I know what you're thinking, "Turn back on your trail you fucking idiot, you're on cross country skis!" And I did, and like I said I think I'm going the right way, but the trail is disappearing in snow drifts as I speak. I haven't seen anybody for about two hours, and there were some rangers and other skiers around back by the signs, but I haven't heard a voice, and I sure as hell would like to find the fucking, goddamned, piece of shit, asswipe Loop Road, which I'm pretty sure I should have come to by now. Help me God…again. Benjamin Booth O'Brian, PHD, TD (Total Dumbshit).

Part II
Mom's Recipe Book

Found in Lee O'Brian's top desk drawer shortly after her death. Mother's Day 2008

No kids, this isn't that kind of recipe book. You'll find all of those in the kitchen. I haven't left anything out there. No secret ingredients are missing from the kitchen recipes. All present and accounted for, I promise. The title of this little essay is my idea of a joke. It only contains one recipe, and it's a flawed one at that. It's my recipe for living. I say it's flawed because my life was flawed. I fear yours will be too, but we can always hope. I wrote this down while I still could. I hope it's of some use. That's what I always wanted to be, in my way, of some use.

Step 1: There's always a course of action. Whatever the circumstances, whether they are personal, political, or spiritual. There is always something you can do. There's no guarantee that what you choose to do will be the right thing, but I come down on the side of doing something as opposed to doing nothing. Your father always felt that was my greatest strength and my greatest weakness. He often believed in leaving well enough alone. Between us, maybe you got the right mix. I'm no judge.

Step 2: You don't always have to tell people that you love them. If you do it too often, they might start thinking that you're protesting too much and that you really don't. Some things should be taken for granted. I hope you always took for granted how much I love you all.

Step 3: Don't have too many heroes. Heroes are human. They are flawed. They are deeply flawed. It's good to admire, but not to worship another person. That's only for God.

Step 4: Work harder than anybody else you know. Never let it be said that you shirked your duty. I believe in duty. It's seen as corny now, I know, it wasn't to your dad and me. We lived through the depression and the great cataclysm sometimes known as World War II. We raised three kids, and none of you were easy, especially the boys. Sorry, but it's true. We had to work harder than anybody else to keep you on the straight and narrow. I know the two of you boys think Jen is the real pistol, the spoiled brat. You only think that because she's a lot like me. Nosier, though. Your father thought she was funny as hell. And he had a great sense of humor. Anyway, work hard. The results may not please you, but the results certainly won't please you if you don't try.

Step 5: Believe in something greater than yourself. I think it's a tragedy if you don't believe in God. If you don't, I frankly don't think you're paying enough attention, but that's your concern. If not God, then an idea like justice, or honesty, or art. Or why not your kids, or somebody's kids. If, like many in this family you're a teacher and you can get a whole classroom full of kids that sustain your belief in them during the course of a 30 or so year career, you're ahead of the game. You've done very well. It's terrible not to believe in something or someone. If you don't, then what's the point of any of it?

Step 6: Don't tell everybody your secrets. Some things should be shared with only a few. Maybe only one. It's okay, when you go, to leave a few mysteries. Think what a special gift they'll be for someone, someday, if they find them out. Think how ordinary they'll be if everybody always knows them.

Step 7: Go easy on yourself. If you're anything like me, and you are, you will spend a good deal of your life thinking you're not measuring up. And the truth is, that may be one reason why you succeed. But it's not the only reason; it's not even the primary one. You're succeeding because you're good people. Know that's true. (Also, be careful how you measure success. Look up Emerson on that. I don't have time to quote it for you.)

That's it. That's all I've got. Maybe if I had written this when I was younger there would have been more. Maybe it's good, then, that I didn't write this when I was younger. Mix these ideas together in a life of purpose. Stir gradually and continually. If you think you've gone wrong, go back to step one and repeat, often.

Goodbye.

Part III
Dad's Hunting Journal 1962
From the hunting journal of Jim O'Brian
(Father of Ben, Jake, and Jen)

     J.P., Lon, some of the professors from the college and I went out to the camp to deer hunt this morning. Had to hike in through snowdrifts. Got a fire going and fired up the oil furnace. Cozy. Storm hitting very hard with northwest wind 30 miles per hour by 5 a.m. Camp seemed pretty nice, and we all decided it was no day for deer. However, a funny thing happened which must never reach my wife's ears.

Lon noticed that ducks were landing out front of camp. It was the only spot on the lake with no wind. J.P. had the idea. What if we just took the front basement window out, like we did the day before, to put the boats in the basement? Then we could throw out decoys and hunt, out of the weather, with the furnace blazing right from the open window hole!

So, by 6:30, we had the shutter off and the window out. Lon, J.P., and I settled down in the basement, while the rest of the crew made pancakes. We set out decoys on the edge of the lake and right in the front yard. By 6:45 we had buffleheads, bluebills, and oldsquaws coming in in dozens! We took 20 in all. Seven bluebills, eight buffles, and five oldsquaws.

By suppertime, and with the window and shutter back in place and nobody but us the wiser, we had duck gumbo cooking on the stove. All it took was Lon's wife's recipe, and a trip to the market. You never know what a day at camp will bring!

Part IV
Meeting Grace
An Overview

They were 19 with all that entails. She, Grace Houseman, an only child, had come north to the Upper Peninsula of Michigan a year before from Grosse Pointe Park on a great adventure with her boyfriend who was a blue collar type form Royal Oak. He was going to be a cop, attending classes at the Northern Michigan University, law enforcement school, she was pre-med at Hunter Hills College two hours to the east of Marquette and NMU. The plan, such as the plans of recent high school graduates are, was they would go their separate ways during the week and meet to ski and love on the weekends. They loved. They skied about four times, until he decided he didn't like the snow. She decided she did, and they parted ways. Her parents wanted to know why in the world she was staying in the frozen north and why didn't she come back to civilization now that she had that low life kid and the low life in general out of her system, after which, she informed them at Spring Break that she had never particularly liked civilization and she was going back north at least until Christmas. She didn't return to Grosse Pointe until her son Michael was born 12 years later.

When she was 20, during the fall of her sophomore year at HHC, she met this clueless, self-important, but charming English major, former football player, outdoorsman, U.P. and Hunter native, Ben O'Brian, in a psychology class. He tried very hard to impress her with his knowledge of Freud. He had very little.

"Um…O'Brian, is it?" she'd said brushing her long dark hair away from her eyes in a crisp wind, as they were walking across the quad together on the way to lunch.

"Yup."

"You don't know shit about Freud. Besides, if you want to impress me I'm a Jungian."

That had pretty much sealed it for him, because, though he was typically unaware of this, she had talked to him exactly the way all the women in his family did. And since the attitude seemed familiar, he thought it was friendly. Luckily, he was right. Anyway, Grace wasn't going to fall for his shit. In the previous four or five years, there had been plenty of girls who had, and therefore he had quickly moved on from each knowing that nobody who believed that shit could possibly be worth staying with. Besides, Grace was drop dead gorgeous and had eyes like a bobcat. As he got older, as is in evidence elsewhere in this text, Ben got somewhat wiser.

As for Grace the fact that Ben thought her forthright nature was endearing was a definite plus. Most guys she'd known did not share this attitude. The fact that he guilelessly laughed at her when she got particularly castrating, disarmed her, and was one of the main things that made her stick with him. Besides, he was smart and funny, and was broad at the shoulder, though he got quite dumpy underneath those shoulders over the years.

All of this led, very gradually, because both these kids were being careful about their hearts, to the inevitable day, the following Spring, when Ben brought Grace home to meet the memory of his dentist father, who had died of cancer five years before, the very living and intimidating presence of his mom, his sneaky little sister, and his elusive brother Jake. As Grace was fond of saying of Jake, "You gotta watch that one." He was never clear on why she said that, until years later, on her death bed she explained to Ben when he asked her about her standard comment concerning Jake, that once when Ben had invited Jake to campus for a little brother's weekend, he'd made a pretty sleazy pass at her.

"What did you do?" Ben asked her on that dreadful last day of her life.

"Before or after I punched him in the nuts?"

It was the only laugh they had that day, and it ended with Ben crying.

But on that first visit 25 years before, Ben's mother had liked Grace, almost immediately sensing a kindred spirit. And she'd let the young couple have some time alone by the fire, honestly believing she was taking nine-year-old Jen with her up to the camp. However Jen, a determined reporter even then, snuck back down to get the scoop, which she did, by placing herself on a bank just down from the camp amidst the birches and by so doing getting her first look, albeit a moonlit shadowy one, at a young couple making love. Interestingly, up to that point the young couple had not made love, because Ben was nowhere near as worldly as he tried to let on, a trait Grace loved in him. And so, for a while that night, they sat alone platonically, on a homemade bench by the beach fire.

"Sorry about the bugs."

"You didn't invite them. And I knew they might show up."

"Still… You know swimming sometimes keeps them away."

"That right?"

"Yeah, hard for them to bite underwater."

"I'm game."

Ben was truly shocked.

"Really?"

Grace was already taking off her sweatshirt.

Ben was quickly with her and followed her as she ran down the short sand beach out into the water and dove in naked at the dropoff, which was just 15 yards out. They swam out 30 yards seeking each other in the half darkness. Then rolled together underwater like otters and surfaced breathless and aroused. The loons suddenly called out to them.

"We're too loud." She said when they heard the calls.

"Shhh." He said and pulled her close feeling the water work it's way in delightful eddies between their limbs. He kissed her, pulling her dark wet hair away from her face as he did so and she moved very close wrapping herself around him. "I love you." He said.

"I know" she said.

"I know you know."

"I know you know I know."

"Now cut that out."

And again they kissed, entwining in the shimmering water.

"Oh my…" said Jennie, from somewhere in the birches.

"Jennie!" called Ben's mother.

"Oh shit!" said Ben.

Grace stifled her laughter against his wet chest.

"Ben?"

"We're…we're fine Mom," Ben said, in a cracking adolescent voice.

"Oh," his mother said looking at the clothes on the beach. "Jennie, you come with me!"

"Up here, Mom."

Jennie was getting a head start to her bunk where she would spend a night with plenty to think about.

From that day, there was never a waiver between Ben and Grace. Oh, there were fights, some dandies, but they were always battles between loving adversaries. There would never be a split. Only death could do that and did.

Part V
Grace's Letter Home

Oct. 2, 1978

To:
Peter and Margaret Houseman
Grosse Pointe Park, Michigan

From:
Grace Houseman
Room 215 Richards Hall
Hunter Woods College
Hunter, Michigan

Dear Mom and Dad,

Well, I know you think it's past time for me to stop this crazy quest in the North and now that Rick has written me to make it clear that he is officially and finally out of the picture, (by the way, quite an ego on that guy I haven't spoken to him since June) I'm sure you think, as I may have implied, I'll be coming home to stay at the end of this semester. Quite the opposite.

I know this summer I led you on a bit with talk about staying near home for school after I got some basic courses squared away here this semester and using Dad's contacts to move right up the ladder, and I apologize for that. I hadn't the heart to tell you the truth. I have never really liked Grosse Pointe. There's something in me that is simply repelled by the sight of all those boys in their Izod shirts and deck shoes. And don't get me started on the girls. I'm only half kidding.

Seriously, all through high school I never once felt in sync there and I seriously doubt I would feel any more at home as an adult. It just isn't me, and it never will be. Now, before you start thinking this is some kind of attack on your moral fibre, our upper class lifestyle, or some such, please know that nothing could be further from the truth. I appreciate all the advantages I've had and continue to have because of your love for me and hard work in getting where you are. I didn't speak my true mind to you about it this summer because frankly, I lacked the fortitude to bring it up. I just didn't want to fight with you about it. Again, I'm sorry.

So, here's the deal. I'm staying here. I'm going to look for a job here this summer. I may stay here throughout my time in college. I hope you'll visit. I love it here. I love the slow pace of life. I love the piles of snow. I love the brilliant, brisk Falls. I love the chilly Springs. I love the Northern Lights and the bears and the ducks and geese and the deer herds that walk right through downtown (for lack of a better description) Hunter. I love the folks here. Yes, even with all their wool, flannel, and toques. (I know, what's a "toque"? You'd call it a stocking hat. The word is sort of pronounced "chook" like "spook" around here. I'm told that west of here, around Marquette, they pronounce it like "brook". Anyway, long story, which doesn't matter.) I love Hunter Woods College, my professors and my classes. And this summer I'm going to get to see what folks here say are spectacular sunsets and sun rises in the warm weather. I'm staying. That's final.

Now if that means the money supply is at an end, well, so be it. I'll make it work somehow. I love you and appreciate you for all you've done, but my home is here now.

Take care. Your loving daughter,

Grace

P.S. There's another new wrinkle. I wasn't going to bring this up, because I feared you'd think this is the real reason I'm staying. I won't deny that it is part of the reason. It may become a bigger part of it. I'm not sure yet. I've met a boy. He's a local. His name is Ben O'Brian and he grew up right here. His Mom's an English teacher and his Dad, who passed away when he was 14, was a dentist. He's smart and funny and a little full of himself, but he's very kind and wonderfully good looking. He's a writer. He's a pretty good writer if you must know. I may be in love with him. By the way, he's the one that filled me in on toques.

Part VI
The Feather Story
As Told by the Spirit of Grace

The Grace who was me then, was busy that morning. It was a cool, cold really, clear June and I needed some time to put together a breakfast. I needed my Ben, and my children out of the house for one hour. I loved them so, but for me to do this breakfast, they needed to be gone.

So Ben took the two of them outside with our golden girls: Snowshoe, our golden retriever, and Minnesota, our yellow lab. Michael wore his big floppy hat to keep the sun off his face. He burned, (ah, remember sunburning?) so easily, and Katie in a cute little toque and my denim jacket that she loved so much. So strange that people love clothing. What the other me used to call fetishism really. So, my lovely little band headed off along the beach. There was a lot of beach that year. Sand. Sand was wonderful. Little bits of life, little bits of earth, the spirit meshing with it all in colors I could almost see even then... I didn't know... I didn't know.

They walked all the way to the other end of the lake at Ben's ridiculous quick pace. He goes much more slowly now. Worked their way past all the cabins off to the east past the two big red glacial boulders, past the stands of oak and maple and fir trees, under the high banks and all the way to Sandy Beach... So cute, "Sandy Beach". Across that channel, that place between, where all the dogs' ashes go. Where my ashes went, not because I really wanted it, but because Ben did and at that point, after all those three had suffered for me, what did what I wanted matter? Ben was right anyway, it is lovely in every way. The shallow water flowing through there from the springs in Mud Lake; the beavers building and rebuilding dams there; the dark water mixing with the light; the tannic acid disappearing in that channel and flowing out to where it was 100, 150 feet deep. There are much worse ways for your earthly self to fade out. Much worse ways.

They took off their shoes and left them on the other side of the channel the two little kids and my big boned husband and the silly dogs, working their way down along the cedar highlands at the front of the peninsula and to the very spot where Ben knew the eagles always perched.

And was there an eagle there that morning? Well, you know there must have been or there wouldn't be a story. And he was there looking down at them as they passed under and he got up, and started to fly away and one tail feather came loose and started to drift on the wind, and well…there are two ways you can tell this story from here. There is the way Ben and Kate tell it in which Ben says, "Catch it, Mike." And Michael, cute as can be, eight years old in his little hat goes running through the water and catches it in his outstretched hands and comes back holding it and looking up at his dad like he's holding the Holy Grail, or there's Michael's way in which he doesn't see the feather and his father runs and catches it.

During that summer when Ben lost himself down on that desperate beach, after the kids had moved away, and he tried so hard to bring me back from here, Michael faced Ben down with the story and told him it was a twisted illusion and that Ben had put so much pressure on him about the story that it was ruined forever for him. He maintained, that the story was ruined because Ben had insisted that Michael had caught the feather. He said that Ben claimed the story was a metaphor about Michael's supposed impending greatness and had made him think something great was about to happen and it never did. Michael said that his disappointment in himself, and fear of Ben's disappointment, came close to ruining his life. Maybe Michael was partially right, but mostly I think he was wrong because whether Michael caught it or Ben did, there is magic in the world and most of it is natural and what absolutely did happen, *what did happen,* is that Ben looked at his kids and said, "Do you see kids? Do you see why your father loves the natural world?" And there were tears in his eyes, and Kate said, "That's not natural Daddy, that's super natural." That's the truth. That's the truth that lasts, even here. That's the truth I don't have to forget because it's at one with the bigger Truth: Love. Just love.

Part VII
Grace is Gone
The Football Game
Kate's Version

Dad and Michael were in the yard. The funeral and the wake were over. Everyone had gone home, except Aunt Jen who was sleeping inside on the couch. She'd wiped herself out caring for all of us that day. Uncle Jake was somewhere in Asia. We hardly knew him anyway. We were sitting on the front porch on the old porch swing. It was early November. November 8 to be exact. I was still wearing the dress from the funeral, a black jumper with a lacy white blouse beneath and my new low heels. My hair was pulled back with a barrette. It was long, even longer than now. And very dark, just like Mom's before she went gray. All of us were cold. None of us cared. Nobody was saying a word. Dad was holding a football. I don't know where he'd gotten it from. Michael hates football, of course because Dad had been a football player. Passive aggressive kid, then and now. So hard to know him. I was one of the few who did or does. Anyway, Dad tossed the ball to him and for once, who knows why, he was interested. Michael tossed it to me and I got interested too. All of a sudden we were headed for the side yard. Dad was running out for a pass from Michael just beyond the big elm. He caught it and ran to the other end of the yard. We followed him. Michael went off to the side of the yard parallel with Dad and lined up like a wide receiver. I got down like a running back behind Dad.

"Hutt one," Dad said as though taking the snap, not a trace of a smile on his face. He turned and pitched the ball back to me. It was hard running in those shoes, and I knew Aunt Jen would have a fit if she saw me, but I didn't care. It didn't matter. None of it mattered. Not the two years of Mom's terrible illness, non-Hodgkins Lymphoma; not the six months of trips back and forth 111 miles from Hunter to Marquette General Hospital; not the eulogy in the form of an elegy which Dad had somehow gotten through without completely breaking down; not the condolences, which though heart felt didn't mean anything at all to a little girl, though they would later; not my seventh grade classes, which I was somehow passing with flying colors to the wonder of my teachers, (really it wasn't so hard, what else was I going to concentrate on?); not my stupid clueless friends who weren't talking to me (I understood that later); not the lonely nights when I didn't say anything to Dad because I knew he was hurting as badly or worse than I was, this being his second time around through this particular cancer nightmare, the first with his dad when he was just about my age; not all the years ahead that would come and go without my quiet calm mother who loved me like soil loves a little oak. All that mattered was that my weird brother and my weirder father were running in front of me blocking invisible tacklers, and I, in my girly black jumper and lacy blouse and new heels was going to score a goddamned touchdown.

Part VIII
The Beach Time
An Overview

So, the thing was, the kids had moved out and Ben, without knowing it, had gotten himself pretty lost in the last six months. He'd moved in early Spring out to the camp and hadn't been back to Hunter since. Jen was worried, but then she was always worried, or at least interested. She and Mark moved out to the camp with Ben as early as they could, considering their jobs and other family complications. Their sons Collin 18, and Sean, 20 were both on their own. Collin, an actor, was working as a barista, between college classes at Northern Michigan University, in the Marquette area, and Sean, as a "zipline guide" in a little place called Saluda, nestled between mountains on the North Carolina-South Carolina border. So the move was easier than it might have been, for Jen and Mark, but it was an imposition. Neither minded much.

An imposition that Ben was unaware of, along with almost everything else but his fixation. And what was his fixation? He believed, or wanted to believe that he was talking to Grace down on that beach. He was eating, what little he was eating, there, sleeping, what little he was sleeping, there and generally living there. He was only leaving the beach to go to the woodpile and occasionally, as a way of bathing, swimming out very far into the lake, sometimes in the dark.

"He's going to die... He's going to die..." Jen said one morning near hysterics staring out at her brother through the picture windows of the camp's front porch as he swam out well beyond the raft into the middle of the lake.

"He's a good swimmer," Mark said from over the kitchen counter which opened onto the porch.

"'He's a good swimmer?' That's what you've got? Seriously? You with your degree in psychology. You who counsel prisoners on a daily basis to keep them from killing themselves or to give them hope, or to keep them from killing somebody? 'He's a good swimmer?'"

She turned back towards the lake. "I'm going after him!"

"No you're not. You'll both drown. Then, when you're both dead, he'll be so mad at you."

"I'm going in a boat."

"And why is he going to get into the boat?"

"Because...because he's my brother."

"Jen..."

"What? What mastermind? You got a better idea?"

"Yes."

"What?"

"Leave him alone."

"We've been..."

"Then let's leave him alone some more. You were right to come out here. We're near him. If something goes really wrong we'll be here."

"He's..."

"He's what? Sleeping on the beach? Building campfires? Going for long swims? Sounds like somebody trying to work something out doesn't it? And in a fairly rational manner, I might add, especially compared to my usual patients..."

"You've heard him. You've heard him. He talks to himself…
Jesus Mark it sounds like he's talking to Grace and he stops as
though he's hearing answers."

"What if he is?"

"Well…that's crazy!"

"Who's to say?'"

"Oh don't give me that philosophical mystical horseshit!
'Who's to say?' Talking to somebody who isn't there is crazy. I'm
sorry but it's crazy… And what's more he's not your brother!"

"He is though. As far as I'm concerned he is. And he's my
best friend in the world."

"Okay, okay…" She calmed down a bit. "That's fair. That's
true but…I don't see him! Where did he go? He's…"

"He just dove. See?" Mark went around the counter and
went to her at the window. "He's headed back. Let's go bring him
some coffee. We're here to make sure that nothing happens to your
big brother and that's exactly what we're going to do."

"Yup. Yup. Okay. I'll get the coffee and a towel."

Jen tried everything. Mark tried waiting and watching.
Sometimes she forced him out onto the beach in the middle of
the night with a six pack of beer with the marching orders, "Here's
some beer, go bond!"

It led to some pretty funny conversations. But Mark was
worried too and without Jen knowing he had checked around the
camp, and around the house in town for the whereabouts of all the
family guns and knives. Like in a lot of rural homes in America, it
was a long list. When he'd checked for them all, even interviewed
the clueless Ben about how many family guns and knives there
were, there was one item missing, Ben's prize buck knife that he'd
inherited from his father, Jim O'Brian. He was pretty sure Ben had
it in his pocket, which was natural enough considering that he was
living on the beach. Still, it worried him.

And one night three weeks later, after Kate and Michael
had come to camp for the weekend, Michael caught his father
holding the open blade in front of his face and looking pretty
intently at his right wrist. Michael, in what to that point may have

been his most grown up moment, took the knife away from his father. Ben promptly gave him the knife forever.

This was the night they had it out about the feather story, Michael holding that it was Ben who had actually caught the feather, and that the damned story was the cause of all kinds of pressure he put on himself and would his dad please cease and desist from talking to his dead wife, attempting to kill himself, and telling that damned stupid story over and over until it became some god awful family myth.

Ben looked up from the lake, at his son. He thought of it all and started to cry. He realized that as much as he wanted his conversations with Grace to have been real over the last few months, in some sense they just couldn't be. They couldn't be allowed to be. Not if he was going to be this good boy's father. Not if he was going to be Kate's father, not if he was going to be his silly sister's brother, not if he was going to be a brother to Jake however distant, not if he was going to be a true brother to Mark, not if he was going to go on living, writing, teaching out the four years he had left before retirement, not if he was going to continue to live.

"Mike. Michael, I'm sorry." And he took his reluctant son into his arms and after a moment Michael wrapped him tight too, but didn't cry, just wasn't in him, but he felt it. He "felt it real" as Grace used to say to her husband, and her children and her patients.

"You've got to allow yourself to feel life. Feel it real. Understand that you're in this moment. Know that you're here for a purpose even if you feel you have to invent one. I don't care if you're an existentialist, a transcendentalist, or a Methodist, you have to be in life and feel the grit under your finger nails and cry the tears and open yourself to hurt and love and all of it."

When she would start in on this, especially that last time on her deathbed, five years before what the family came to call, "The Beach Time", Ben would nod and cry. And when she saw the first tear she usually stopped, but not that last time. She said it all and he wept and wept. And then she kissed him for the last time there in her hospital bed in the front room of the house in Hunter. And because of that moment, Ben was okay to get the kids through what kids have to go through and out of the house for good. And after that was through, finally, the details of life fell away and the big loss of the love of his life dropped right down and swallowed Ben whole and sent him to the beach where only the swimming and the fire building and the talking to his dead wife and ultimately his family, especially his holy fool of a son, could save him.

Part IX
The Bizzaro Ukrainian Wedding
and Mike's (Michael's) Brilliant Idea
As Told By Jake O'Brian

It was a hell of a thing, my wedding. A traditional Ukrainian wedding in the least traditional spot in America: Reno. Shiny. Just shiny. It started with an absolutely hedonistic bachelor party made so by my wife Christy's Newfie cousins and uncles. Ironically enough, all of them were from the Sault Ste. Marie, The Soo, most recently. They'd left Newfoundland to take jobs with Algoma Steel. Christy had never been in the U.P., thank God for that because if Ben knew she almost did come to the U.P. once and why, he'd kill me. Anyway, I knew exactly where these guys were from. They loved that. Maybe a little too much. When they heard Ben, the best man, did I tell you they don't take that idea lightly in the Ukraine? Well, we'll get into that... Anyway, when they heard he still lived in the U.P. I thought all three of them were going to have heart attacks. Eventually the Newfies started talking about going down to the train yard and hopping a freight to California. Ben and I went with them and we ended up in a freight car drinking ouzo straight. Ben and I bailed before the bottle was gone and called a cab. The three of them ended up in the pokey. I bailed them out and shot some legalese at the cops who thought the whole thing was pretty funny. I thought we were out of the woods, then the reception started. When Christy told me about the best man thing, I thought she was kidding, but she wasn't. She explained the grand march and told me I had to get somebody to look out for Ben. Thank god Mark was there... But the grand march...the way it works is they line up shots of every kind of alcohol you can possibly imagine on one long table. Then everybody who drinks, and at a Ukrainian wedding that's most everybody, walks by and chooses somebody in the wedding party with whom to drink a shot. And, the best man is considered THE BEST MAN!!! and must drink with everyone else, and consequently much more than everyone else. Shiny, right? So four shots in Ben looks at me and under his breath while still smiling at all the nice people wishing Christy and me well, says, "Are you kidding me with this shit, Jake? I'm 60 years old. I don't want to insult her family but…"

Right then Mark pipes up, "Tell 'em you're only drinking vodka."

Ben, still smiling says over his shoulder, "What the fuck difference is that going to make?"

"Trust me," Mark says.

So, when one of the crazy uncles stops through and says, "Ben is the Man!" and crosses arms with Ben and says "Nostrovia!" Ben tips back the "vodka" realizes its water, deadpans it to the uncle. Then he says on the Q.T. over his shoulder to Mark, "You're an unholy genius! Vodka into water, our wedding feast miracle! Thank you!'" Ben became a legend in Christy's family that night. And I never told anybody the truth about it. Still, we almost got caught because one of the more educated inlaws from Chrity's family, Uncle Phil, I think from Washington State, drinks a shot with Ben, leans in and says, "That's water isn't it?"

Ben says very quietly, "Yes. Gonna rat me out? Have a heart, I'm too old for this!"

And Phil says, "Hell, no. Just wish I'd thought of it when I was best man." He grins and walks away.

Well, interesting things were happening all over that room. Over by the ballroom door Kate was talking to a willowy middle aged woman with a bearing not unlike Grace's, though I hope not a left uppercut, (God, that still hurts), who later was revealed to be the mystery woman from the train. Christy had to dance a dance or two with her old boyfriend…Michael who seemed more than fine with the whole thing, but I caught Ben eyeing them up very suspiciously and so I walked him out on the front porch for a cigar.

"You sure you're up to this?" He says to me when we get out there. Meaning Christy being 32 and my being 55 I guess.

"Shiny." I said lighting up the stogy.

By that point Ben had had enough actual shots to ask me something pointed.

"What's with you anyway? 'Shiny' what is that bullshit, just a way of not telling me anything about your life?"

"It's worked so far."

Up to that point he had looked pretty angry, but now he started to laugh.

"Okay. Okay. Shiny it is. Serves me right for asking you a direct question. And it's your wedding day. Never thought I'd see it. Why now though…after all this time?"

"Love."

"Really, you?"

"Yup it's…"

"I know, 'shiny'. Asshole. I'll give you a pass."

"No, really, she's just special. She's a translator. Don't know if you know this but Michael introduced us.

"He did?" Ben shot me a pretty intense look.

"Oh, you know he's always going from place to place, running and skiing and writing about it? Well, he met her in Tibet of all places, and he told her what I did and that maybe he could get her a job connected with my work… So one thing led to another."

"Wait a minute," I saw the suspicion rising up to realization. "Were Michael and Christy…"

"Oh, oh, no no, I don't think so. At least, Michael never said so."

Ben was staring right at me, hard. The way he used to just before he used to pin me against a wall.

"Christy would have told me. It's shiny. I swear." I shot him one of my patented grins, fully realizing that those grins rarely worked on him. Suddenly I realized I had a trump card and that I'd better play it before I got my clock cleaned. "So what's this I hear about a woman on the train, reminds you of Grace?"

Ben starts to say about five things. Three of them maybe cussing out Jen for telling me his business. So I know I've hit the right cord. He's forgetting about the other thing. Then I see that crooked smile of his and he looks me right in the eye.

"Shiny?" I ask.

"Shiny," he says, and shakes his head.

I looked over at Christy's parents. Sitting holding hands in the corner. Tough old birds about ten years older than me. Jane was part of a cattle family from way back, Mick had been a hired hand. He grew up in a one room house in Montana. Friendly as can be both of them and tough as nails. Whatever Christy wants is okay with them. But, between you and me, Mick scares me even more than Ben does.

Later in the haze of the early morning hours, just after the Newfies disappeared for parts unknown amidst shouting, the sound of, I think ,a flugel horn, and the crashing of some plates in the kitchen; just after I saw Jen and Kate having a fairly animated talk over in the corner by the punch bowl in which they both kept looking at Ben, Kate smiling, Jen shaking her head; just after I saw Mark, for the millionth time calming Jen down and urging her, I assume, to just stay out of her brother's business; and just after Jen told me what she thought and what she knew about Ben and this woman and that it was my responsibility to talk to him, and just after I said, "Ben'll be fine. It'll be shiny" and Jen said, "Oh sure, it will be shiny. It will be shiny because as usual I'll do what I always do and bail all you lunatics out!"; and just before Christy and I finally took off; I saw Ben and Michael huddled in a corner and every couple of minutes one of them would say something about big trees and the Mariposa Grove. By the next morning both of them were regretting the plans they'd made to head off in Michael's rolling office, otherwise known as his mini truck with a camper (which I bought for him, don't tell his dad), to go backcountry skiing in the Mariposa Grove in Yosemite. Each of them told me later, separately, that they each wanted to tell the other that this was maybe not the time, but didn't want to admit it, and before either of them knew it, they were on the road leaving Ben to reschedule a flight and pay a little bit extra. Still, as things worked out, it was probably worth it. It was all part of the plan. Shiny.

Part X
The Near Drowning Story

(Jake's wedding reception, just before the private talk between Jake and Ben. Sound of voices, including raucous laughter, jazz music, silverware on china plates, footsteps. Jake and Ben are standing surrounded by a number of young men and old from across the country.)

"Okay, so Jake, I know you think this story is about what a big doofus I am, but, in my version…"

"In your version ha!"

"In my version you don't look so good. "

"Okay, okay, so get on with it."

"Okay, so Jake shows up at camp with his big friend, the President of Afghanistan or something…"

"Oh jesus! Good start…he was a…well a district attorney for Cabbal…"

"Okay, somebody important from Asia."

"Ha…okay…okay go on."

"So he shows up with this mucky muck and wants me to show them a good time, during duck season, so I give them the good boat. Not to mention that I set up the decoys the day before."

"He doesn't tell you that he leaves the damn things out all season…illegally I might add."

"'You might add…' whatever. Anyway, I had them all set up and sent them down to the good blind. Then I went out in this riverboat that I knew was unsafe and hadn't used in years for that for reason…"

"Oh, what bullshit! When have you ever, ever been concerned with safety…"

"Ha, okay, okay, just sayin'…"

"Just sayin'…"

"So I head out on Mud Lake..."

"Yeah, that's the name. We grew up in a really sophisticated place."

"Hey, we've got a college in town!"

"Yeah...Hunter Woods College...built on a bluff and operated on the same principle..."

"Okay...I'll let that slide. Anyway, the wind had started to come up and I had that little motor in reverse right into the east wind that was blowing. And I don't know it because I'm wearing my hip waders, but water is pouring in over the gunnels."

"Perfectly understandable if you're the kind of airhead this guy is. And this was 20 years ago! Senility wasn't even a factor yet..."

"Okay, so wait. So, I start down the lake with a boatload of water and all of a sudden the bow is pointing straight up in the air! And I'm going, 'Jesus, there's a hole in the boat!' And I start trying to figure it out. Did I put in the plug..."

"Oh come on! Admit it! You just panicked!"

"Okay, sure, sure that's true. I won't deny it. So anyway, my dog Shoe bails out and she's swimming to shore and I look over and figure. Seems reasonable. So instead of staying with the boat..."

"Like Dad pounded into our heads over and over and over..."

"Right, so I try to swim out..."

"In waders!"

"And I start to sink and down I go. And I went down three times. And the third I thought 'I'm going to die.' And then this little voice says..."

"Here we go with the little voice...He's always got a little voice..."

"The little voice says, 'Roll over on your back and an air pocket will form under your coat.'"

"Very specific little voice!"

"Good thing."

"Yeah."

"Anyway, sure enough I float to the top and make my way

to shore. So about this time, Mr. Yosef…"

"Wow! Impressive! You actually remembered his name."

"Okay, so notice it wasn't my brother who noticed something wrong with my little boat. Anyway, the man gets my idiot brother to turn around and come back. And when he sees the boat floating without me in it in the middle of the lake, does he worry I might be dead? No. What he says is he turns to Mr. Yosef and he says…"

"'What did my idiot brother do now? Ha, ha, ha! Oh my god, so funny!'"

"See, he admits it… What a piece of work…"

"Shiny, shiny. So then Ben hollers for me from where he's standing drenched and frozen on the shore. And I look over there and holler back…"

"'What the hell are you doing?' Not, 'Are you okay?' 'Are you alive?' 'What the hell are you doing?'"

"Ha, ha, ha, ha, ha… Yosef was so upset he wanted to rush to Ben's aid…"

"Yeah, because he was a decent human being unlike you…"

"Like a little mud water was gonna kill ya…"

"It was 30 degrees! I could have died… I'll be damned… I've been dodging bullets for years…"

"Oh, look the professor is getting all philosophical now. Uh oh. Uh oh. The waterworks might be coming… what a baby!"

" Huh…oh screw you Jake. Anyway, so okay, so guys… guys…be honest. Who looks worse in this story?"

"Ha…I think the consensus is pretty obvious, bro!"

(Raucous laughter all around.)

Part XI
A Lovely Rescue
Michael's Version

There was Dad. There was Dad. I was so mad at him, and I love him so much. He'd almost knocked me unconscious, then he'd

listened to my ravings as I yelled at him. I figured he'd just go for
a quick mile around the parking area while I recovered, but, as he
explained it, "I just followed the trees." But there he was, there he
was, my dad, his burly frame coming at me out of a near whiteout,
and saying, as though he hadn't been scared to death, "Oh Mike, oh
Mike. Those trees…they're so beautiful." And what he was really
saying was, I'm so sorry. I'm such a fool I didn't mean to scare you.
I love you.

It all started with my backpack. He insisted on hauling it
out for me and I told him not to. I had just set my skis up against
the side of the camper and I came around to the back door just
as dad was swinging my backpack through the door. The metal
frame of the pack caught me right in the nose, the back of my
head slammed against the open camper door, I slipped, went flying
straight up in the air, came down on my head and lay there in the
snow. For a second he didn't even realize what he'd done, then he
saw. And he says, "Mike. Mike. What did you do?"

"What did I do?" I said. "What did I do?"

I went back into the camper grabbing the backpack away
from him as I shouldered him out of my way, tripped and fell again
bouncing my chin off a cabinet. "Dad," I said without looking up.
"Why don't you just stay out there, or maybe even take a little
warm up ski, just for a little, while I collect myself." Then I saw my
nose in the mirror and felt the lump on my head. "Jesus Christ…
Dad, Dad just go for a while, okay?"

"Mike, you okay? I mean, sorry. I guess…"

I looked at him pretty hard and he read it. He's good at
reading it, not so good at reacting.

"Yeah, okay. I'll ski a bit. See you in a half hour."

"Kay."

Well, I was okay in fifteen minutes or so. Then a half hour
passed. Then an hour and the snow started to pick up. So I geared
up and followed his tracks. I thought of how this whole thing
started. All Dad and I ever want is to be okay with each other and
we really are, but what we say always gets in the way. Sometimes
I just want to tell him, "Dad, everything is not about you! Yeah,

you've been hard on me. Yeah, you probably pushed me sometimes in ways that were pretty over the top, but it's not always about you. Sometimes I'm just a fuckup, and I have that right! I have a right to my own fuckups just like you do, but what happens to me isn't always your fault! It's not all about you." I don't know, would that be a good thing to say or not?

And I thought, what if this stupid outing were to lead to something really bad? All this from a stupid deal we made when we were both drunk at Jake's wedding. That would be just so, well, stupid. Sometimes I think Dad and Mom and Aunt Jen and Uncle Mark and Kate and, well, everybody is right when they say you've got to watch out for Jake. Even though, and don't tell Dad this, he has funded about six or seven of my outdoor expeditions, and bought me the truck and camper, though the shoe and gear companies are paying me pretty well now and I am getting quite a following. But, I mean, he did kind of steal my girlfriend, which is a little twisted when you think about it, but that's not exactly what happened. Yes, we were dating when I introduced them, but really, I'm not much different from Jake that way. I was getting kind of tired of her... The way she expected me to, well, kind of be there all the time and not just take off. And the stuff about always calling her, responding to texts, remembering stuff. Well, that was getting old. So when we had that dinner with Jake in San Francisco, and I could see she liked him, I just point blank asked her that night, "Do you want to date my uncle?"

And her face went red and her eyes got big and she took kind of a breath and said, "Um...yeah."

"Okay." I said.

And then, do you know, she really got mad at me? Who can understand women?

Anyway, I'm moving along this snowy track in the middle of nowhere in Yosemite and I'm barely making it, and if I'm barely making it, how well, tough as he is, can Dad be doing? And the snow is getting heavier all the time and I'm three hours into the chase at this point and really I never would have forgiven myself. Never. After all of it. My breakdown, his breakdown, Kate's breakdown, and Mom. Always Mom at the center of it. Well. It was great to see the old man coming my way. And I hugged him and he said, "Oh Mike, oh Mike… Michael. Those trees are so beautiful."

And I said, "We're never doing this again."

And then he laughed and he cried.

My dad's a funny guy, you know?

Chapter 9
Mystery Woman at the Wedding

So…I think I met Dad's girlfriend at Uncle Jake's wedding reception. I was standing there in this beautiful ballroom: parquet floor, oak tables in neat rows; white linen table cloth, tasteful china, dim lights; getting ready for dancing, to jazz yet. David and I had flown here from Michigan. Dad was standing with David now, having a beer with Mark at the mahogany bar at the far end of the room. Truth is, I hardly know Uncle Jake. He's been traveling the world my whole life doing work with new democracies on their constitutions and legal systems, on behalf of the federal government. What kind of work exactly? Indoctrination? Propaganda? Legal technicalities and procedures? Who knows? For a while, when we were very young and loved adventure, and later when we were left wing paranoid in college (Well, when I was in college; Michael flunked out.), Michael and I used to think Uncle Jake was a spy. He's closed mouthed enough for it, but he's entirely too goofy. Then again, who knows, it might be a good cover… Nah, nobody who says "Shiny" all the time could be a spy. Who could forget that? And thus he wouldn't blend in well. Sometimes I think he says that just so he can be remembered. Not sure where he picked it up. Michael says it's from the short-lived sci-fi TV series *Firefly*. But I doubt Jake ever saw it. I did get Dad hooked on the Firefly DVD set, but then he wanted to analyze its likely literary and cinematic root sources, in one of his informal lectures, and took all the fun out of it.

Anyway, back to Uncle Jake. He always acts like he knows me. "Hey kiddo, how are things? Shiny?" All that stuff. And I guess he does know me. He's at least known of me for a long time and I seem to remember that he was around more when we were younger. I remember swimming with him when we were little. I vaguely remember skiing with him in Banff, Alberta on some trip with Mom and Dad and whoever Jake's girlfriend was then, fashion model from Africa I think, when I was little. But who can be sure? I was pretty young then. No, I really don't know him. Anyway, he certainly knows me better than I know him.

Truth is, I don't think Dad knows him much either, except the way you know people from growing up with them. I know Dad used to get really mad at him sometimes when they were young. That's what Grandma said anyway. She said it got physical the way it does with boys sometimes. I even heard once that Jake made a pass at Mom. And Mom, ha, Mom punched him in the nuts. Ha! That would be Mom.

When I think about it, the way Dad knows Uncle Jake is kind of the way I know Michael. Michael is always out and about and never around Dad or David or me, and well…we all know he's an odd one. Not in the same purposefully aloof way Uncle Jake is, but similar. I kind of think Uncle Jake, pays for a lot of Michael's outdoors journeys and running treks too. Just a hint or two there, and Michael's not good at hiding anything. Doesn't really see the need. Poor guy is really socially inept. A touch belligerent about it at times. Anyway, it's not just the companies and his cyber fans paying the tab for his journeys. That's okay. That's really okay if it's true. I'd like to think Jake is that nice a guy and not just a womanizing asshole who says, "Shiny!" for no particular reason. The thing is, family is family. Whatever works. I'm not sure the whole, "Well, she was my girlfriend but you can have her" thing between Michael and Uncle Jake is that cool, though. Good thing Dad doesn't know about that. Oh, yeah, it's really good Dad doesn't know. I guess if Christy's okay with it…

She seems nice. Her family too. Weird juxtaposition of

things though, a Ukrainian family comes to Montana, becomes cowboys. Two generations later one of those Ukrainian ranch hands, who by now has forgotten what it is to be Ukrainian, marries into an old cattle ranching family, but boy the relatives come out of the woodwork and go full bore ethnic when there's a wedding if this is any indication. The wedding ceremony was something, and oh this crazy reception... Poor Dad. It's borderline dangerous how much they're making him drink! It's like frat boy stuff. And he's 60. As I understand it, though, Uncle Mark figured a way around it for Dad. Now, Uncle Mark...there's a stand up guy. I'm amazed he and Jake haven't sparred a time or two. When they were young I bet they did. I can't see Mark putting up with that kind of nonsense. Aunt Jen has always seen the good in Uncle Jake though. She's always really nice to him. Much nicer than she is to Dad. Truth is, though, she respects Dad. She wants his approval, but can't bear to let him know that, so she teases him all the time. Of course Dad dishes it out pretty good too. They're funny together. You can see how much they love each other. As for Jen being nice to Jake, I think she's always been afraid somebody is going to clock him, and figures if they see that she likes him maybe that'll keep Jake from getting a black eye. I'm not sure he really needs her help on that score, though. That Jake, he's got a line a mile long.

Anyway, I'm standing by the door looking up at my family, thinking how much Dad and Uncle Jake and Aunt Jen look alike as they sit up there at the wedding party's table... By the way, it's pretty funny seeing all the old farts on Jake's side of the table and all the young people on Christy's. It made for some funny couples coming down the aisle. Again, Christy seems okay with it... Anyway, I'm standing there by the door and this woman, lean, pretty, late 40's with graying dark hair that she has not colored, looking like, well...Mom.. stepped up next to me and said, in a voice that was uncanny in its approximation of Mom's, "That's your family on the right hand side of the table isn't it?"

"What?" I said, a little shaken by the sound of her voice. "I mean excuse me, I'm sorry I didn't hear you."

She smiled at me, seemed quite at her ease, "On the right

hand side of the wedding table, your family?"

"Yes. Are you with Christy's family?"

"No…" then she seemed a little uneasy. "Just a guest at the hotel, passing by the door."

"Then…how did you know it was my family?"

"Oh honey, you all look just alike! Your hair is a little darker though."

"Well… they're old."

"Ha, true, and by the way I'll try not to take offense at that…"

"Oh," I said and laughed. "I'm sorry, but you…you don't look old…I mean…"

"Hon, don't hurt yourself." she said and laughed. "What's real is real."

"What did you…" That really threw me off. I couldn't help thinking of Mom's "feel it real", which confused me when I was young, frustrated me when I was eleven, then made me cry alone in my bed after she was gone while I was in high school. I remember saying into the night once when I was 17 and a boy had broken up with me and Dad didn't know what to do, "Did I really have to feel it this real, Mom?" Anyway, the turn of phrase, the look, and mannerisms and the voice, uncanny. "…I didn't…"

"But the two men, the groom and the best man," she ways saying, "…seem like they must have been blond once. The best man gave a great toast! He's very literate."

"Well, it's kind of occupational. He's a poet and an English professor."

"Is he also your Dad?"

I nodded, dumbfounded at this point.

"And the woman down one from your dad, she's your aunt?"

"Wow, you're good." This seemed suspicious. How could she possibly nail it that exactly? I started paying very close attention.

"I travel a lot."

I looked straight at her and I think she could see I was about to start asking my own questions.

"Figuring out people and their connections...passes the time," she said, and suddenly she just came completely unglued. I had absolutely caught her, she thought, and she tried to make a quick exit. Actually, I hadn't quite connected it all just yet. Anyway, she got this "what-the-hell-am-I-doing" look on her now blushing face, said, "Sorry, oh, have to meet someone," and she was quickly gone.

It took me two seconds to remember what Aunt Jen had told me when she met David and me at the airport the day before: "Some woman your dad doesn't even know, who apparently looks like your mom, kissed him on the train!"

"Wait, what...Where?"

"In the observation car!"

"No, I mean, on the lips? It wasn't just a friend of his or something. A buss on the cheek?"

"No, no. This was like a strangers in the night love thing! They practically got naked, I think, or some such. And then she just disappeared!"

"So you weren't actually there? Aunt Jen..."

"Katie, I swear! He told me so himself!"

"Dad...told you...himself?"

"I was amazed too. He's kind of well...happy about it."

"I'm going to have to ask him myself."

"You don't believe me?"

"Of course, but Aunt Jen, ya do exaggerate sometimes..."

"Okay ask him! Ask him! Her name is Valerie. Travel agent. She's from Iowa. Two daughters. Divorced. Ask him! She just kissed him and disappeared. Doesn't even know her last name, but he told her *his*, the damned old fool! She could be a stalker! Anyway, ask him!"

Well, I hadn't, because when I thought about it, I figured if he wanted me to know he'd tell me. But it seemed Jen did have the scoop this time and now what she'd said came back to me as I stood there trying to make head or tail out of what had just happened with this Mom clone. Without thinking, I said out loud right there in that ballroom, loud enough so a couple people heard and I blushed, "Oh my God, that was her...Valerie..."

Well Dad, I thought. *She seems really nice.* And then I thought. *How did she get here so fast? Had he invited her? Were they sharing a room in the hotel and he hadn't told anybody? That's kind of sweet... Oh God. No. That's not it. She's a travel agent. It would be easy: a couple of inquiries; wedding in town; O'Brian; easy to get the plane ticket, discount, frequent flyer. That was the mystery woman! What would Aunt Jen do if I told her this? I can't. I just can't. Oh...ha...I have to! It's too good. It's too absolutely wonderful! Dad's happy. This cute woman has a thing for him. She's really sweet and vulnerable and just couldn't stand to be away from him! My daddy's got a girlfriend! Like I'm not going to tell Aunt Jen what I know. It would be cruel not to tell someone like her. She lives for stuff like this. Besides, she's always, ALWAYS, had our best interests at heart and Dad wasn't hiding it from her. And it's not going to do Dad any harm. It might even get them together faster.*

So, Dad, I'm sorry, for better or worse, so to speak, I did it. I told Jen. And she went absolutely nuts! It was so funny! I hope I haven't "admitted impediments to the marriage of true minds", but Aunt Jen has done right by us so far, and I know you trust her too. Let's see what magic she can work this time. Ha, ha, ha!

Chapter 10
Lake Stories
With Commentary by Val

So this is Ben O'Brian's book of poems, well, one of them. Got it off Amazon. Not a big seller, but a rare opportunity for somebody blatantly scoping out a man she met on a train. God, I'm so ashamed…so stupid. His daughter was so sweet. And she's no dummy. Got a 3.9 in undergrad. Editor of the college literary magazine. God, I know she knows who I am. And soon the little sister will. I hope I haven't killed it before it even starts.

Oh, this is crazy. I shouldn't have started to begin with! What's happening to me? I haven't felt this way in 11 years. More really. All my friends have tried to fix me up. Told me I need to get over it already, move on. Do I want to be alone forever?…all that. And now this. This is just out of control.

He did look…well…just great standing up there giving that toast. He's so articulate. So learned. Wow. I like to read, but he's big time literate. Shakespeare, Chaucer…

Oh, come on. Those old dead white guys are on your bookshelf too. Come on! You can hold your own girl. Listen to me, my own support group. The question is, do I want to hold my own with him in literature? Do I want to just hold him? Do I want to? Do I really want to?

And he's retired! Retired! That means he's at least 7 or 8

years older than I am. Oh, from the bio 12, lovely. He didn't look it though. And some of the pictures of him make him look young. Well, maybe he was, they could be from years ago...so creepy girl!

Retired. *Now, to be honest, he didn't say that. Probably set in his ways, though. And big red flag.* **BIG RED FLAG,** *why hasn't this been uppermost in your mind:* **YOU SOUND LIKE HIS WIFE HE SAYS.** *You remind him of his dead wife. Expectations, expectations. Do you want to be a stand-in for somebody dead? Really, really.*

Turn the damned computer off. Switch to Pandora, Facebook, shots of Fiji, anything. And put this poetry book up on the shelf before it's too late, or give it to a friend, or a customer bound for Antartica or...

Huh...the students really liked him. "Charismatic, but a little opinionated." Oh this one says "asshole." Ben probably flunked him. Still, 'opinionated', well he's a teacher for god's sakes and a poet. Of course he's opinionated. People pay for his opinions. He seems to have good ones, so what's the problem?

Old curmudgeon? Could be...but probably, no definitely from the sounds of his poetry and what he said to me, leftist. Fine with me, but wouldn't the family love that...oh god...a leftist college professor conversing with my uncle Herb, or his son Rick the county Republican Party chair? Girl, switch to another site or turn off the computer.

YOU REMIND HIM OF HIS DEAD WIFE!!! And now I'm haunting the family! Hanging around at their weddings LIKE I AM THE GHOST OF HIS DEAD WIFE! What is wrong with me?

Whatever may come of us, if anything, if I ever even contact him again, or he contacts me, I am never going to get him out of the Upper Peninsula of Michigan. It's there in every poem. Every single one. It's his life's blood. If I want him, I guess I'm going to have to want the U.P. and specifically that lake. And all those trees. And his family...even his dead wife.

Anyway, the poems... This first one, the title one, really sums up how connected he is. His "little sister" her name's Jennie, two years older than me by the way, must have put a crowbar under him to get him on that train. He's got a brother, Jake, the one who's got married. Big deal international lawyer, works in third world democracies for the government. It was easy to find him on Goggle, pictures with the President, international leaders. Very handsome...Ben didn't mention him when we talked. Jealous of him maybe? Ashamed? Hmmm... First marriage at 57, bet he's left some broken hearts... Ben's son is a writer too. Looks like his mom, I think.

Grace was very pretty. And very smart. Wow, near top of her class at Michigan medical. And she ends up in the U.P. which means she loved it too. She may have loved it even more. She chose it. I hate that I've done this...I don't seem to be able to stop.

Lake Stories

Lake Stories
Stories that float on this wet essence
Between the cool ridge pines
And the insatiable cattails.
Stories of this cold, clear lake.
Stories that flow over gravel bars
And under wet bear paws.
Stories that drift in the colors of dawn over northern waters.
Stories that disappear in the ebony of new moon,
Wax to full with August's passing,
Age around beach fires that speak
In maple growls and birch whispers
But never drown the sound
Of the water's relentless rush to shore.
Stories we tell to our children
Who huddle close near us in the sand
And conspire with each other in
Way-past-their-bedtime glances.
They listen, as we did, to ancient tales,
And beg, "Just one more, please one more!"
O those stories:
Of wild uncles, wiley aunts,

Grandmothers, grandfathers,
Sisters, brothers, cousins,
Old friends
With names like "Stitch", "Bump", "Dale", "Buck", and
"Shine."
Loped eared dogs with wise eyes central to canine tales all
their own
And Mom and Dad in inconceivable younger days
All mixing then and now with
Wolves in the hemlock wood,
Deer so close our laughter quickens their ever startled
hearts,
Porkies gnawing the cedar shakes,
Beavers tail slapping warnings to quiet us,
Sandhills drumming, chortling their flight call,
Loons trilling and wailing in the darkness,
Coyotes celebrating in the valley far across the water,
The squeaking wings of buffle head ducks,
The comic quack of mallards,
And the haunting calls of Canada geese in morning mists.
All part, all paragraphs, sentences, words, syllables, songs,
In this story we, here, have been writing
Since Kingfisher first dove from a tamarack branch,
Eagle first eyed the northern air,
Fox first found his bristled den.
Always, these lake stories
Reflected in the emerald of your eyes too, love,
On this cold night
By the fire,
By the water.
This one lake story we have made here,
You and I.
That many have made here,
Of feathers and quills, agate stone, and pine tar,
Composing those old words,
Washed in the light and dark waters of our mother love,

Our northern dreams,
These lake stories.

Oh God. I'm going to cry. I'm crying. He loved her so
much. They were so very good together. So obviously in love. They
were all mixed up in this place where they lived. I can't be that. I
can't ever be that. And the fact that I remind him of her… That's
just so hard. Impossible. And now I've let myself be known. His
sister is probably going to contact me soon and ask me what the
hell I'm doing and I wouldn't blame her.

He loved Grace so much. Well. Well, I'll just have to talk
to the sister. Tell her how much I think of her brother. Tell her
I couldn't help myself. If she's as big of a snoop as Ben says she
is… Well, she should understand. But oh…I can't be Grace. I just
can't be her. He'll know that. He'll understand that, but will that
disappoint him, at some level anyway?

What Bears Do

The little bear
Up on the high sand bank
Was doing what little bears do.
He was maybe a year into this world
Still open to new bear things
When I came along
In my canoe.

And what do little bears do?
Well,
From what I could see
From my tipsy vantage
Early day on the water
Was that little bears watch
And try to figure, as best they can,
(and sometimes that doesn't go so well)

He was sitting there
Front paw cross over front paw
Sitting back like a short legged man
Watching his favorite football team
(The Bears?)
on his couch on Sunday.
Minus the beer, of course.

I see I've made him too cute
As we always do when the true wild is too mysterious
As it always is
For our little human heads.
So I'll just add this and try not to presume too much
About bear thoughts:
This little bear, high on the bank under the birches,
Was looking at something he'd never seen before.
It was strange to him
I'd guess.
I doubt, in his bear mind,
He separated man from clothes from boat from paddle,
And it all smelled so strange
Anti-septic. Soapy,
Not at all of these north woods

He looked at me,
I watched him.
And then he'd had enough,
For a bear still fairly new.
He slowly walked up the bank,
His nose still lifted
His naïve eyes still focusing
On the strange thing
In the water
As he vanished above the bank
Into the woods.

He was gone
Off to do what bears do
After they have seen some things
Off to walk the woods
With something to remember
Open to a new bear day
Open to all that bears must do.

Okay, does every one of his poems make you cry? Or is it just me? What am I turning into here? A poetry groupie? This one is just…precious. So cute. He even kind of admits it's over the top. Hate to be a critic but this is probably not great literature. Does have some insights though, about how arrogant we are. And not for a second do I miss the reference to his kids. "What little bears do" well…precious…

My Sister, The Moon

My sister, the moon over the water,
Watches me rise early to hunt and fish and paddle.
She catalogues my foibles,
Arbitrates my inward squabbles,
Hears me mumbling and humming in the boat
In the crystalline dark.

She shines out clear over calm, cold waters.
Plays hide and seek when the clouds come,
Coy, flighty girl.

She is married to the dawn
Who speaks in his time
In his wide, red voice across the horizon

She is a good wife to him,
Seeking always his best interests in her darkness.
Taunting and teasing his grandeur

Just before he comes.

She humbles men
Reminds them with her wisps of mystery
Of the reasons for their darker longings.

She is the haunting light.
She makes the shining path
On still nights,
Which all men wish to follow.

She leads the way through the dark,
Wickedly wonders aloud in a voice of light
Just what we men would do with the ebony delights
She hides, just beyond the black.
And having silently said just enough,
Leads us back to day and all
That must be done.

Well shit. He really loves the women in his life. Unless
he's just talking about the moon here. No, this is the sister. I talked
to him for twenty minutes and she came up as somebody pretty
important. Somebody he was trying to avoid talking about, but
couldn't. Important enough to get under his skin. I get the feeling
it's love hate with Jennie, but it's mostly love. This is a tight family.
Good lord. His family and my family. What would that wedding
be like? My family would insist on a big wedding... Would his?
Church and all? And he's Catholic. Hmmm... Uncle Herb detested
Kennedy. Whoa girl. Way ahead of yourself. And that sister is going
to come after me hammer and tongs, especially now that she knows
I was at the wedding. Why did I push it this far?

The King

I had a dream once, right here, under this old quilt.
Well, actually I had that dream tonight. But it could have

been any night
Out here.
And in that dream all the good men I'd ever known
were standing along the rim of that valley
behind the lake.
In a mist, under a full moon.
We were all dressed as ourselves.
Some in business suits,
So engrained were they in what they do.
But most of us dressed in leather jerkins
Frontier caps
Holding flintlocks.
Oh, some had broadswords and kilts.
Some were in baseball spikes
Cradling gloves and balls
Wielding bats.
Some looked into the distance
Others straight down at their hands
Wondering, knowing, smiling at the chances.

I won't pretend it doesn't sound funny
As I sit here endlessly comfortable again
In the camp under the quilts
Thinking about where the bass might be biting
Come dawn.
But then, for the purposes of that dream
And make no mistake, dreams have many purposes,
It was all real.

All we did was know in that dream.
All we did was nod to each other in confident glances
We lack everywhere else.
We knew exactly who we were
And why we were there.

The king was coming.

Real as the dawn
The king.
No, not Elvis,
THE king,
The one we've always been waiting for.
The one who pulls back the hood,
And tells Robin of Loxley that he's Richard,
Back from the crusades
All will be well.
The one who wears a million hoods,
A million masks,
That perfect father,
Brother,
Son,
That
One
Male
Self
That makes all well,
All still in that valley
He was coming.
And we were all there rallied to his cause.
And then, of course, just as the battle cries rose,
Sounding from each masculine mouth,
Unique and joined in righteous promise

Of justice and safety and freedom forever,
Just as all those hunters and warriors and wizards
And ball players came together in that wondrous
War cry
Just as the king emerged from the forest
Just as he almost raised his regal head,
I woke, under this old quilt.

Alone, contemplating papers,
And meetings, and days full of drudgery

that waited down the road
Outside these old woods.
And then, a thankful thought:
Not today! Not yet, today.
And so right now I roll back over
To renew my summer dreams.

Tough outer guy with a soft heart. That's obvious the moment you meet him. At least it was to me. And the imagery here, the men under the moon, in the valley: substance. Men who aren't just suits or tractor operators or old jocks. Knows his place, his purpose. Ha, he has a purpose. More than you can say for a lot of men. Heck of a friend in a fight I think. And knows how to choose a fight. Wouldn't make that choice lightly. You know, his poetry is a little pedantic, always writes like he knows something you don't, like Frost, but he is a teacher. He does have a message. He's sure of something, several things, so why shouldn't he teach what he knows in his poetry? Just a good man.

Damn it.

It Comes Back

And so, it comes back
After the wind and the water,
Fire and snow
After everything I know and knew once about hawks and eagles,
Bear and bobcat,
Wandering moose
Ridiculous otter
After all that and myriads more
It comes back to you.

You with your hair like the whirling fires of my oldest dreams.
You with your words like the pine clear whistles of osprey

Over a shimmering bay.
You with your eyes like cold clear water
Over old rock deep.
You with your arms like oak wind in September branches.
You with your hands like birch roots in winter sand.
You with your breath like spring wind in the jack pines.

You to whom I can't say goodbye because you never go.
You who will always haunt my best wishes as I watch the
sky
Out city windows and schoolhouse doors.
You who will always come to me unexpectedly,
Like a doe serene and wondering on a wooded path.
You who breathe my name cajoling, convincing, confusing
In my interrupted sleep.

Here

On this earthly peninsula
Between midnight and moon
Here in this late summer storm as I huddle by the fire.
Here in this isthmus between madness and daylight
Here where I wait for you knowing the answer
Knowing you can't come here
And will never leave
Knowing my old heart
Is in for ever more aching
I prolong the time between
Cherish even the pain of your absence
Long for long days that can't come
Perfumed by the presence of your smile,
Enveloped in the music of your laughter.

Too much. I should stop reading now. This just makes me
sob. He's hurting so much or was when he wrote this. I could sense
that pain when he talked to me. The loss of Grace is his every third

thought, still, I think. Would I be enough to fill that void? Do I want to be? Either I just can't dare to insinuate myself into this man's life, who loved this wonderful woman so much... either I just need to stop now, right here, right now, or I need to go in... ha...loaded for bear.

I can't ever be her. I can't ever try to be her. I have to make that clear to him right away. It's not his fault, but I just can't let him ever believe that I am agreeing to be her. Is this relationship even possible? He loved... He loves her so much still. I've just got to write it off, I think. It's just a whim, isn't it? I need to stop caring for this man I hardly know! But how can I not care for a man who cares for a woman this much?

The Mysteries

It's never as simple as it seems,
Or always is.
Our dreams are half truths we tell ourselves
And are told from outside our inside
Inside out.

To shout the words before we're sure
Is dangerous folly
To wholly know is the goal:
To drink ambrosia
And eat nectar

To know the stars as friends
And take only as much note
Of beginnings and ends
As befits those loving tricksters
Life and Death

Breath is not made of air
Nor Earth of dust
All trusts must be tested

And thus all tests will disappear

To hear the colors of all the suns
Of men and gods
Is to be finally not at odds
With what is and will be

To need tragedy
To weep at birth
Is the meaning of all
The Earth and Cosmos

"To shout the words before we're sure is dangerous folly..."
Ouch. That seems like an accidental warning to me to be sure I
want to do this before I take one more step, let alone crash a family
wedding. "Accidental"? Not if there are no coincidences. At some
level maybe he is warning me now, even though he wrote it then.
Oh brother, that's philosophical, or just bad science fiction. Still,
this poem seems to say "Val, you need to try."

I need to try to know. No need to shout about it, just find
out. Huh, now I'm doing it too. His poetry is contagious, the way
he messes with sound and sense. I'm taking on some of his traits
just by reading his work. So maybe It's all one. So, I look like her,
sound like her, and I met him on a train in the middle of nowhere?
Can that be an accident? I'm sure he doesn't think so. And you
know what? I don't either. We seem to have so much in common.
Even a common mind set. But what will I do? What will I do...
Ha, it's a mystery.

Fire

It draws us, doesn't it?
Especially late, by the water.
It makes us know things we've always known
And didn't know we knew.

It's always new
And ancient old.
It keeps out the cold
Beside these somber late summer waters
Until dawn glows
Like the coals
And fire laughs his last.

Then
Young voices wake the sun
For play by the lake.
The water is getting cold.
But we take is as it comes.
As the wind does
Clearing off our old leaves.

Quickening, this lake breeze
Scatters all.

And so
we collect what's good that's left,
Put it in our old pack sack
And head downwind
Until these waters warm
And this old fire
starts again.

I like that: "collect what's good that's left, Put it in our old packsack and head downwind". Well, Ben O'Brian, I've got a packsack. I'm collecting. Will I have the guts to go where you are? Where's my atlas?

Chapter II
Grace is Okay With It

If you're worried, don't be. I'm okay with it. Jealousy is ridiculous here. All those little conflicting emotions you all worry about, just as I did? They don't exist here. They smooth out. Jealousy? I can't really remember it anymore. We were lucky though, Ben and I. We never slipped. Not even close really, either one of us. So there's that. But really, to be jealous is ridiculous, immature, and ego-centric there too. Can you make somebody keep loving you by demanding it? If a man or woman you love has thoughts about anyone or anything other than you, does that make him or her unfaithful? We're human. Sometimes we stray from a true path. Sometimes we just waver. That's not to be condemned. In one sense perhaps it's even to be celebrated. It shows a person is alive and aware and capable of pulling himself back on a true path, and sometimes not. That's beautiful and tragic. That's human. I very vaguely remember having this conversation with patients.

Whether Valerie Traeger looks like me or sounds like me is really not that important. If my voice and my looks still attract the man I will always love, then if I were still that other self I think I'd be flattered. But she's not me. In her best self she knows that. Jen knows that. Ben knows that. Kate knows that. It's almost a game they're all playing. They already know the outcome. It's lovely and silly and human. It will be all right. I have a sense of something really good about to happen. Something quite special. And all these people I love, despite myself, all those people I still love specifically, are involved. That has to be good. And I think whatever this will be will allow me to step away a bit more, even a lot more. It will be that kind of good. The water of life forms a wave, you know. It comes and casts some things, ideas, people, away, and takes others with it. It's a wave and a mirror and music, music and of course none of those things really. Again, the labels make it all go away. Those old nouns are the most human of words. Designed to pin things down, stave off death by identifying what we have, even invisible things like empathy and courage. When we're alive we're so desperate to pin things down. Hold on to them. If we could only learn while still alive, that releasing, letting go, in jealousy or in grief, is the only solution to our despair. Freedom, folks. Freedom.

Ah, but it will be good.

I don't mean nobody is going to die, or get their heart broken, or run crazy. I don't know really. Truly I don't. That's a linear thing. All that's irrelevant here. It's an illusion anyway. Time? All that? You were this age, then you're that age, and you're getting older so you better start exercising. Age. What a dumb thing. If you're 3 or 93, you don't really know much. And yet you know everything if you can only stop moving and searching. If you could only stop thinking and listen. But my dears, you can't. I love you all, but you just can't.

Not yet.

But it will be okay for Ben and Val and Jen and Kate and dear Michael, and Jake. And Huck and Tom and all the other pups from all those years, well they've always been okay. Always will be because they're in the now and in the know in a way live people can never be.

Feel it real folks. Feel it real.

Oh…I'm going away…goodbye.

Hello.

Chapter 12:
Jen Isn't

"SHE CAME TO THE WEDDING!?" When Kate told me I screamed that out loud. Sometimes I'm a fool. Mark has told me that; not in so many words, because, *he's* not a fool but he's told me that. Ben *has* told me that in so many words, so have both my sons Sean and Collin because they are all fools like me. No, I'm not clueless enough to think that I never get out of line. I know sometimes my big mouth and my nosiness cause everybody in the family problems, but come on! I had a right to yell. She wasn't invited. She didn't even contact Ben to ask him if it was okay, though that big doofus probably would have been delighted.

Come on! Who is this person? Who does that? She's a damned stalker! I haven't found anything in her background incriminating yet, but I'm going to keep looking. There must be some crazy in there somewhere.

Of course, when I told Mark that the woman had been at the wedding… Yeah, I know, me and my big mouth again, should have left him out of it, poor man! Anyway, when I told him, he said, "Who told you that?" He thought I was imagining things or making it up. When I told him Kate had told me, he stopped smiling and just nodded. "Huh," he said.

Typical man! "Huh." As in, "well, that's mildly interesting, isn't life funny? Good to know" not "Jesus Christ, what in the seven dark hells is that skulking harpy doing at Jake's wedding?" So clueless.

Then he asked me a hypothetical…Do you know what he said? He asked me, "What if she's just in love with him?" Typical man! So egotistical for his sex. Yes, Mark, I thought, all women just go around the world every day mooning over every verbose, overweight, self important, 60-year-old teacher-poet they see!

What I actually said was, "Like a nice looking woman 12 years younger than Ben is just attracted to him out of thin air, on a train in the middle of the night?"

Oh, then my lovin' husband, Mr. Smarty pants, what does he say when I said that? He says, "So, let me get this straight, she stakes out trains looking for little known poets? That's your theory? Did she make herself up to look like Grace too? Does she only stake out little known poets whose wives have died?" Then he shook his head, acting like I was nuts, and walked out of the vestibule at the reception hall, where I'd pulled him to fill him in.

Well, okay, I admit it, that did give me pause. Even if he did look so smug. But I don't care what anybody says, she wants something. Nobody can see that but me! By now she knows he doesn't have much money. She knows he's a poet… that's it, she's a groupie! She may have been following poets for years. She reads their books and then thinks they're magically writing about her or something even worse! Maybe she's got a whole list of little known poets she's bumped off!

Well, maybe not…

If Ben hadn't run off like an idiot with Michael to go ski in the Redwoods, maybe I would have had a chance to talk some sense into him. Then again, if I told him about her being at the wedding, he might have gone straight to Harbinger, Iowa, the old fool.

Now there's a name! There's a name! "Harbinger!" Trouble literally written all over it! Harbinger of doom! Dammit! Dammit! Ben you big fat doofus!

If he does find out she was there that's just what he's going to do. I can't tell him what I know. Oh…that's gonna kill me… If I tell him that'll just send him there faster. Maybe I can tell him and get him to see it the way I see it. He's got to see the reasons I'd be worried. Yeah, like he's ever listened to me before.

Oh, he'd probably just pat my little head and treat me like I was 7 and say, "I can take care of myself you little sneak." And then if I got mad and told him I wouldn't let him go, he'd set his jaw and say, "Try and stop me!" Or worse, he'd say, "Please don't hide in the birches this time," or something smartass like that.

He might even take the high road and say, "Did it ever occur to you that this really isn't any of your business?" Is he kidding me with that? That would really bring the old Catholic guilt into play though. He knows how to use that, just like Mom did.

Maybe I should have just kept it all to myself so that when this all goes south I could sidle up to him, comfort him and then deliver the ultimate I told you so. Tempting, but I'm not that much of a bitch.

Should I tell Ben or not? I asked Mark late that night in the hotel room, and do you know what Mr. psychologist said? "I'll leave that to you and your conscience." God I hate him so much right now!

WHAT DOES THAT WOMAN WANT?!

Chapter 13
A Long Trip Home

I got the phone call, while riding in a cab in San Francisco, a gorgeous city I'd never seen before. Everything was so good. So full of promise. I'd had that weird and wonderful adventure in the redwoods with my son, who really seems to be coming into his own, despite all the mistakes I made with him, the pressure I put on him after his mother died. He looks good. Seems to know just what he's doing. As I understand it, his next stop is Machu Picchu, where he is going to run up the mountain into that impossible ancient city, then write about it. Better him than me. I'd be terrified in those heights, probably get lost in the ruins, old ruin that I am. Anyway, he took me out to dinner at some fancy place the name of which escapes me, like most everything in that great city. And keep in mind that "great city" comment is coming from me. We had a great steak, as we sat there eating al fresco, looking out at that wonderful bay. Well, I had a wonderful steak, he had the sprouts or some such. I saw three or four beautiful girls eye him up while we were sitting there, including the waitress. Takes after Jake that way, but doesn't seem to know what's going on around him. Certainly isn't working any angles with them as Jake most certainly would. But Michael looks good. He is good. He may be a Holy Fool, but he's a fine looking specimen of one. Our boy. Grace's and mine, and now very much his own. That's all I ever asked for him, I think: autonomy, independence. You'd have to ask him about that I suppose. When we finished eating, we drove out to the airport. He was going to help me make arrangements for a flight. I told him it wouldn't be necessary.

"How come?"

"Well, I'm not going straight home."

"Oh," he said. And honest to god, he was just going to say goodbye and get on the plane without asking me what I meant. I've gotten used to this with him, he just doesn't pick up on cues. Social interactions are so tough for him. Or rather, tough on the folks he fails to have them with. Folks like me, and those girls, and a million others he's never met because he literally doesn't have a sense of their urge to speak with him, interact, be people together with him. When he was little the teachers wanted Grace and me to have him tested. In particular his third grade teacher, Mrs. Jacobs. Nice lady, but a little anal. Okay, a lot. When we got home from parent teacher conferences, the first night the proposition was raised, Grace looked at me and said, "If they keep pushing this, I'm going to use every connection I have in the psychiatric world to have Mrs. Jacobs tested."

I didn't disagree with her at all. We weren't having it, either of us. I never have believed in labels, inside or outside the academic world, and Grace was a rare psychiatrist who believed that people are who they are and that there aren't enough labels for all the ways there are to be human. I think, and I know Grace would agree, that labels, classifications and micro-classifications, are largely what is wrong with the way we live now. "We murder to dissect," said Wordsworth, and I think he was right. That doesn't change the fact, though, that lots of people would say that Michael has Aspergers syndrome. Somewhere on the low end of the scale, Mark said to me once and I shot him a look and he shut up and never said a word to me about it again. I don't know. I just know that he seems happy now, and I'm sure as hell not going to get in the way of that. God knows, I've been in his way most of his life.

When he was young, because I could see how bright he was, and especially after Katie was born I expected him to take on so much. I remember, right after Katie was born, and Grace was still at the hospital, I picked some flowers in the yard and made Mike carry them all the way to the hospital. I shouted at him viciously and admonished him if it even looked like he was going to put them down for a second. And he was just a tiny boy. I was stressed, hadn't slept well the last couple nights for obvious reasons and I put so much pressure on that little boy. And he didn't even flinch. Didn't react in any kind of emotional way. Why didn't I see it then? I just kept trying to make him be the way other people are. I kept pushing on what I thought was his hard shell. I didn't know what the hell I was doing.

That sense of aloofness, of disconnection serves him well as a runner, though. I remember once, when he was winning all the cross country meets in high school by wide margins, right after he'd gotten some brand new running shoes he was obsessed with, he came off the course and said to me, "You know, Dad, my feet kinda hurt."

"Well, let's take a look," I said.

He took off his shoes and both of them were full of blood. He had blisters and gashes on his feet from those new shoes everywhere and he had just kept running.

I remember thinking how tough he was. How tough he'd always been. But I didn't really get it. Not until three years after Grace was gone, and I found out he had flunked out of college in his first semester. I just landed on him like a block of granite. I screamed in his face, asked him what in the world he was thinking. Told him he was in for it now. Took him from business to business making him look for jobs. Waited in the car. He told me later that he mostly just went in and bought packs of gum. Never even talked to the proprietors. Gum. He'd chew up whole packs in a half hour. Hide the wrappers under his bed.

And, oh god, I just kept at him during those weeks after he flunked out, seeing that he wasn't reacting. Knowing how tough he was, I just kept pushing, harder and harder, constant pressure. My anger with him was a compulsion and his stoicism just made me worse all the time, until finally, finally the calm facade just broke, like glass. Suddenly, inexplicably to me then, he was having seizure after seizure, Katie and I took him to the hospital. His head, his arms would twitch and flail and his head snap unnaturally to the side. And I was so terrified. And Katie, I almost forgot she was there. Sixteen years old and looking at me with her mother's eyes.

"Call Uncle Mark," she said, as the nurses tried to hold him steady in the bed, and the emergency room doctor tried to find out if he had a history of drug use. So I called Mark and he asked me how many seizures there'd been. I told him at least 20.

"Over how long a period?"

"I don't know. Maybe, 40 minutes."

There was a pause on the line. "Ben, these seizures are emotionally induced. They're not chemical."

"What?"

"It's good. Or as good as it can be. These won't damage him, but he's got himself into a state. Maybe over flunking out of college?"

I knew right then. I'd done it to him. He wasn't reacting, so I'd pushed him to the point where his constitution just couldn't take it anymore. Nobody's could have. I'd caused this with my stupid, heartless ranting at my own son. I so wanted my Gracie back at that moment. Had she been alive, she'd have seen the dangers. She wouldn't have let me push him so hard.

But now, now it's good with him at least. Whatever damage I did him, I think he's forgiven me. Much more importantly, because as I always have to remind myself this isn't about me, he seems to be holding his own. He looked so glad to see me coming out of that snowstorm in the Mariposa Grove, and at least he knows I love him. That will never take away those bad moments by the hospital bed, knowing that I put him there, but he knows how I feel, I think. I hope. I pray. Anyway, he's on his way, to Machu Picchu. Then there's something else… a marathon in Amsterdam? Something like that. So that's good. And Jake and Christy are off on their honeymoon to parts unknown. So I won't see my brother now for a while. A long while probably. And that's…ha…shiny.

Anyway, at the airport I told Mike I was going to Harbinger, Iowa to meet Valerie. He looked at me absently, for a moment, even though I'd spent most of the drive from Yosemite to San Francisco telling him all about her, I think it hadn't really made an impression. Not much does. But he picked up on it after looking blankly, but intensely at my face, and put out his hand as though we'd just met and said, "Well Dad, I'm happy for you." And then, after an awkward moment, he gave me a sweet little hug. My boy.

I was happy with that. I was really happy. I was in a cab, in San Francisco on my way to the train station to go see a girl. All things that would have seemed impossible even a month before.

I called Dale back in Hunter to tell him I'd be gone for while longer and could he trudge into the camp and check and make sure all systems were go. He told me he wouldn't have to trudge since the snow was gone. "Come to think of it though, I may have to snowshoe by morning. They're talkin' up to 20 inches. Anyway, by truck or snowshoe, I'll give her a check."

I told him all things were great here. On an impulse I even told him that I'd met a woman on the train. He laughed. I laughed. "Well, good luck, Doc," he said. "Don't do anything I wouldn't do. Keep your stick on the ice." We laughed again, said goodbye, hung up. The phone rang. It was Kate. And that was wonderful. I wanted to tell her all about how good it was. With Michael, with me, maybe with me and Valerie, and I was going to talk with her about silly ol' Jen, and see how things were with David and just have a lively conversation with my brilliant, beautiful daughter.

"Hi, honey! Oh this is a good day." I could feel tension on the other end of the line.

"Dad…"

Yup, I thought, too good to last. "What's wrong? You okay? David…what?"

"It's Huck. I picked him up at Ray's…at the sugar shack and Ray said he thought something was wrong. Huck seemed glad to see me and all, but he was limping pretty badly. And Tom seemed really uneasy, like he sensed something with Huck…I don't know. Anyway, we took them both over to our house and Huck seemed to get worse. His whole right side seemed to be ailing. So I took him to the vet. Didn't want to worry you until I knew something."

"Okay…how bad. Did Jeff Jesson look at him?"

"Dr. Jesson says he's had a stroke. Pretty bad one. They watched him over night. They've got him sedated. I've brought him back home. The doctor says he'll be okay for now. The next couple days will tell whether he's going to come out of it or get worse."

"Oh Kate, I'm sorry you had to deal with that."

"I'm sorry Dad."

"What are you sorry for? You've done great. You did just what I would have done."

"Where are you?"

"San Francisco. I'll get on a plane right away and head home."

"Dad?"

"Yeah, hon?"

"Sorry I ruined your day. Are you okay?"

"Oh, hon, that's silly. He's just a dog."

"Uh huh, that the story you're going with?"

I started to cry. Then I laughed. "How did your Mom get into your mouth to say that?"

She sucked in some air, stifling a little sob, I think. Then she laughed. "Hurry home. We'll bring the dogs to the camp and wait for you there."

I told the Middle Eastern cabby to reverse course and head it back for the airport. He was way ahead of me, nice fella. He said, in his pleasant accented baritone, "Sorry, about your troubles," when I paid the fare at the airport.

"Thanks."

Then he was gone and I was going through the motions in the terminal, trying to find my way back to the U.P. and my 12-year-old dog who was more than likely dying. I called Jeff Jesson, while the harried young woman behind the counter was trying to figure my best route. She said something about nothing available at that moment because of a big weather front moving through the Lower Peninsula, snow and freezing rain, but did I want her to call the Air Canada terminal. There was a flight into Toronto, non-stop, then another to Sault Ste. Marie, Ontario. I nodded to her and she wrote down a number and pointed down the terminal. I started walking hardly knowing what I was doing. By that time the doctor was on the line.

"Jeff?"

"Ben, sorry about the old guy. He's such a character. We all love him here. Afraid his hunting days are over."

"How bad?"

"Well, he's a tough old bird as you know..."

"How bad?"

"I don't know, Ben. And that's honest. Most dogs get hit as hard as he did, they'd be gone already."

I took a breath. *This is just a dog.* I kept telling myself.

"Yeah."

"But Ben, I've seen that old boy do some amazing things in the hunting blind. Remember, after his leg surgery? That very next year? You and I were out there at the channel...We knocked down the ringnecks in the shallows..."

"And the one was lively. Your dog Spike grabbed the dead one and Huck took off after the other and it kept diving on him and going out deeper and deeper and the waves were just rolling in..."

"And he just disappeared."

"And we thought the worst."

"And then that old dog, bum leg and all came back through that pounding storm, snow and sleet, horizontal wind, after diving down after that bird four or five times in that chop...And he dropped it at our feet Ben, and looked up at us like he was saying, who's old and washed up?"

"Best retrieve I ever saw from any dog, any age."

"Best there ever was. Who knows, Ben. I'm not holding out false hope, but who knows, he might sleep for a couple of days, then wake you up in the morning with a wet tongue and tell you he's hungry."

"I want to hope so."

"Hope's free."

"Thanks."

"You gonna make it back with the storm?"

"Yes. They've found a way around through Toronto."

And so, before I knew it I was on the plane with all those polite Canadians. Funny, I didn't even think of Valerie and all that until we were in the air. It seemed pretty remote at that point. I could barely remember what she looked like, except that it seemed she was a bit like Grace.

I remembered Grace telling me near the end that I had to keep raising dogs. That the kids would need that. I would need that.

"Okay," I'd said absently, looking at her vitals on all those damned machines, looking into her ashen face.

"No," she said, "you listen to me. You listen. Those dogs are important. They bring out the best in you. Get a good one. A nice big friendly one with plenty of personality."

And after she was gone I didn't get one for a while. I told myself that every time I bought a dog I was just buying a little more tragedy and I felt like we'd had enough. Then Katie told me one day, very matter-of-factly, just the way Grace would have, "Okay, time for another dog." It was a June Sunday after church. We were in the kitchen at camp. She was holding up the classified section of the newspaper. The three of us went over to a breeder in Munising later that day. She picked out Huck for me while Michael was playing with the other pups. Huck was the big fella minding his own business over in the corner under the stairs, while the other pups scrambled over each other and Mike. And we'd brought him home. He never whimpered.

And he'd been so special. Right from the get go. Loved the kids. Loved everybody's kids. Jen had used him in a play or two. And he was the dog in Kate's Midsummer Night's Dream. And oh how the audiences loved him. There had been a moment after one of the performances, this one for a bunch of elementary school kids, when I was walking Huck out of the theatre. The kids were still in their seats, under the watchful eye of their teachers and as I led Huck down the middle aisle they all reached out for him, wanted to pet him. He obliged them all, putting out his head licking hands, just, I swear, smiling at them.

"You're a superstar," I'd said to him.

And then that one time with the blackberry pie Jen made for us all when the whole family was out at the camp. Jen had gotten up early and made it, and she'd caught Huck with both paws up on the table and his face buried in the pie. Oh lord, Jen was so mad and we all laughed so hard until she started laughing too, and Huck, just looking from face to face with the berries dripping down, trying to gauge how much trouble he was in.

What a great dog!

Idiot that I am, sitting on the plane thinking of all this, I burst out crying. And the stewardess came over, asked if she could help. I said, "No, just some illness in the family." I smiled at her and wiped away a tear and felt silly. I was glad there was an empty seat next to me. I pretended it was Grace and smiled at it. Maybe it was.

This wasn't so bad, I told myself. I'd been through much worse. I just hoped I'd get there in time.

Come on old pal
Keep swimming
Keep swimming one more time for me.
Break those waves.
Bring that bird in.
There's a warm fire waiting.

Truly bad poetry. Not good for much but the caption for a picture in *Ducks Unlimited* Magazine.

There was no denying, though, that I loved him. No denying that dogs had been part of my life since I'd had life. That some of my most profound experiences had been with them. Grace had understood that about me. She wasn't a huge dog fan, but she had come to love mine and ours. My Mom could never get that. To her, having grown up on a farm in the depression, well, a dog was a farm animal. Totally expendable. Though she did have a soft spot for some of my dogs. When she was nearing her end a few years back, and I had the caregiver duty one night, I'd slipped away while she slept for a quick shower, keeping the bathroom

door open in case she called out. Suddenly, Huck was there in the
bathroom, having pushed the ajar door aside with his head. I could
see him through the sliding glass door. I pulled it back. His eyes
were insistent. I needed to come with him. Then I heard Mom call.
"Ben…" Amazing dog.

Come on old Pal.

Then I thought of Valerie. And her face did come a little
clearer. Something in all this was not letting her slip away just yet. I
was clinging hard to the happiness I'd felt. She probably liked dogs.
I thought. She grew up on a farm. There'd been so little time for
either of us to know anything. What could I know? What could I
really know about her? Our lives were complicated. I knew that.
Wrapped up with all kinds of family. And all that that entailed.

I thought of all the things I'd done for family. That family
had done for me. Our private football game that meant so much to
Kate on the day of the funeral. She didn't know the whole story of
that. I'd never told her. It wasn't the first football game on the day
of a funeral in our family.

October 30, 1973: Dad had been buried that morning and
Jake and me were still in our suits from the wedding sitting on the
porch. I had a football and I tossed it to him. He tossed it back to
me, hard the way he could and we were off. Next thing I knew we
were tossing the ball back and forth, hard. Then running out for
passes, diving for the ball into the mud. Making a mess of our suits
right there in the front yard on the main street of Hunter.

And Mom called out from the porch, "Boys! Look at you!
People are watching today." Then she turned and went inside.

I wanted to shout, "I don't care if they're watching, Mom.
Dad's dead! Have you heard? I don't care about my suit or my tie
or what the fucking people in this fucking town think, my dad's
dead!"

And of course, that was unfair and even at 15 I knew that,
but I wanted to be mad at someone. So, when Grace died, that
flashed back to me. And for no good reason, I just wanted to play

football, and I wished Jake had been there right then, but he was gone. Caught a plane right after the funeral. But I wanted to show Kate and Michael that I was going to do whatever was necessary. And I think I did in my own very imperfect way.

And how could I ever make anyone who wasn't already a part of our lives understand it all? The deaths, and the football and the writing and the inside jokes? My gorgeous soulful daughter, my crazy sister, my holy fool, colored glass son, and my aloof brother, my mother and father and all they did for me and us on their shift, and my tears right now thinking about this wonderful dog: my friend who was dying half a continent away Even then, even with all that though, I wanted to try. Even at 60, with most of my energies in my past, I wanted to try this. I wanted to see what love with this new person, this Valerie, would be like. I wanted to bring her into my world of love and loss, as my hope for the future. Was that fair? Yes, I thought, because I wanted to share her love and loss, her family out there in Iowa, too. I wanted to know her dreams, her hopes. All that was true. I truly wanted Valerie. I knew that, but it kept slipping away, just as Huck was slipping away by the warm fire my family had kindled by now.

And then I fell into a doze and down the rabbit hole of the tragedies that happen in all families, my dad not himself apologizing to my mom on the forced marches in the snow after he was diagnosed with cancer, home from chemo and half out of his mind, "I'm sorry, Lee. I'm sorry," he'd say. And she'd ignore him and try to say something cheerful. Keep him moving. Walking was good. Me, alone, walking across landscapes that were familiar and unfamiliar into dark woods and out the other side to light that became darkness again. Walking along the lake trying to find a way out of death, trying to find my father and then Grace walking by my side and getting smaller and more skeletal and disintegrating into dust and dry blood with nothing but her smile staying like the Cheshire Cat, and now Mom fading away, telling me to be a good parent, and Michael writhing in the hospital bed, and this time, this time he wasn't going to make it even with Katie and Jen and Mark right near. Then they were far, walking with Jake away, their back's turned and me calling. And suddenly there was a wolf. And I looked up, and I realized I had slept through most of the flight and we were on approach to Toronto.

"No," I whispered. "Sorry, too late. Time is out of joint"

"Little heavy weather, folks, but we'll be on the ground in a few moments," the pilot was saying.

A while later, on the ground, in the terminal, I found out that my flight into the Sault was on schedule and would get me there about 10. I called Mark and asked him for another in an endless string of favors and he just said, "What time, Bud?"

Before I knew it, I had slept, bad dreams about dogs and fathers and sons and mothers and wives and all, through another flight and I was on the ground again and Mark was saying, "Okay, the last leg. Kate says all Huck's doing is sleeping. So that's good, eh?"

"Yup," I said. "Thanks, Mark."

And he gave me a tired wink that said, why would you ever bother saying that?

And an hour and half later I found Kate waiting up for me out at the camp. She and Dave had driven in there with their little truck. The snow had melted down. The thaw had come early this year, while I was away. The road would be good now until the mud made it impassable for a week or two before true Spring finally came in May. That is, barring another snow storm. And now we rolled into the driveway in Mark and Jen's jeep. My truck was parked out by the road. I'd walk out tomorrow and drive it in. I got out of the truck and walked to the door. I sighed once and opened it. I walked inside and Tom met me at the door, with a few whines and his wag tail dance and, I swear, led me over to where Huck was sleeping by the fire. The old guy raised his head and managed to lick my hand. Then as I sat down beside him without my wasting words the two of us didn't need, and I was too tired for, he fell asleep instantly right on my lap.

"Hi, Dad," said Kate half asleep with my volume of Emerson on her lap. She reached over and turned off the lamp above my old chair where she sat in the corner then got up and replaced the book in Mom's massive old fire corner shelf.

"Hi, Kate."

"I guess you can take over from here. I came on shift three hours ago. Jen was with the big fella all day. I've got to work in the morning, but call if you need us. "

"Take care, Bud." Mark said from the door. Then, Kate went into the back bunk room to wake Dave and Jen and the four of them headed out, but not before Jen kissed me on the cheek and offered to stay. "Go home you little sneak," I said.

She gave me a sad smile. I knew what was coming next. "Sure you're okay?

I pointed to the door and managed a grin, "Jen, honest. Love you."

The door closed, then slowly opened again. I waited for Jen's last attempt, but it wasn't Jen. Suddenly Kate was leaning over me her arms tight around my neck, she said, "Dad, it's not always about death."

Then she was out the door.

I sat running the coarse hair of Huck's ruff through my fingers.

I got a little loopy then I guess, and found myself falling asleep with my head against the seat of the armchair and my butt resting on the dog bed. I thought about getting up and lying on the couch, but it seemed like such an effort. Besides, I was pretty sure Tom was already asleep there. And then I felt a little pain in my left arm, and it didn't occur to me that it was just Huck's head resting there. In my half sleep it was pain…with my morbid fascination fully engaged now…on my left side and it seemed like it was moving and now maybe in my chest as I got dizzier and my head kept nodding and well…

I'm too tired to explain
So I'll just say goodbye now
Goodbye to all
All my days and ways
Dogs and wives and fathers

Mothers and Daughters
Men friends and fun with footballs
Wet footfalls of deer on the sunrise beach
Ducks in the October moonlight
Wolves on the winter ice

I could never explain
all the reasons again
So it's easier now
Better too, I hope
To just let this door stay closed
Let the fire go out
Stop the shouting
And just whisper goodbye
to all my seasons

Chapter 14
Valerie in the Storm
A Travelogue
(External and Internal)

Part I: The Predicament

This is her house. This is the home of Jennifer O'Brian-Hicks. The little sister. The one who gets into Ben's business all the time. The one who got him on the train to begin with. The one I have to thank for meeting Ben. Oh, she's gonna kill me! I wonder if she's watching me right now. Looks like somebody's up. Maybe more than one somebody. Jesus, they probably know exactly who I am. What are they saying in there? Or do they just leave their lights on?

Who is Ben anyway? How long did we have together? Twenty minutes tops? Then I saw him make a toast in Reno. Talked to his daughter, who almost certainly figured out who I was and probably told Ben, if not this sister. So why hasn't he got ahold of me? If he is interested at all, like I seem to think, why didn't he notice me standing at the door at the wedding? Then again, why would he think anybody would be crazy enough to follow him to Reno? Maybe everybody in that family, including Ben is ready to kill me....or to welcome me to the family. How the hell do I know? God, this is so crazy. And here I am thanks to Dale.

Did I mention Dale? How did I meet Ben's handyman? Maybe everybody's handyman in this little town? Well, he also drives a wrecker.

Maybe I should start from the top. Anything really not to ring this doorbell at…what…5:45 a.m. in a driving snowstorm, but their lights are on. I guess if it really goes south, I can walk over to the Hunter Fixall Garage again, and see how they're coming with fixing my rental car. Luckily just a slightly dented fender. Dale's friend Rex estimated about $150, which probably means $300, though maybe not in this town. I don't suppose, in a town this small, you'd stay in business long if you were ripping people off. Anyway, I decided to just go ahead and get the work done ASAP, since I might need it today to drive back the 120 miles or so to… Sawyer and the airport. That is, if it all goes south. Not a lot of rental places in Hunter, Michigan. And I'm insured so…

This is so crazy.

Part II: The e-mail to Bunny from Val at the Hunter Fixall Garage

To: bunnysrunnincafe@goletter.com
From: valsouttolunch@nuffsaid.com

Okay, Bun, don't go crazy. And don't tell ANYBODY!!! I'm in Hunter, Michigan, at the Hunter Fixall Garage to be exact. I know, "Where?" You're used to hearing from me from Fiji and Mexico and what not, but why Hunter, Michigan? Well, first, I should tell you that I won't be back for a few days. Well, at least I hope not. Tell Timmy just to forward all his questions to my e-mail and I'll answer as time allows. Tell the family that I'm in Fiji. They're used to that. Leading a tour or some such, say.

The thing is, and I know how hard this is going to be to keep quiet about, I've met somebody. I actually met him on the train a few days ago. Then I went to his brother's wedding in Reno to see him again. Except, he didn't see me that time. His daughter did, though. Nice kid. Sorry. It's a long story. And so far, I think at least, it's a good one, except for the blizzard and the car wreck. See, you're not going to believe this: in the middle of the night on the train, just before I got off home, I sort of kissed him. *It was my idea.* Then I played the mystery woman, and truth, Bun, I kind of stalked him. Then I showed up here practically on his doorstep. Well, really on his sister's doorstep. Well, actually across the street from her doorstep at the Hunter Fixall Garage. That's where I'm sending this from. I'm trying to decide whether to cross the street and ring his sister's bell. Wow, that doesn't sound good. Long story. By the way, there are wolves here. I met one. A real shaggy wolf. Yeah scary. Cool though. Mystical almost. I'm okay, though. Fiji, just tell them Fiji. If the family asks, I'm in Fiji. Make sure it's Fiji. Anywhere else they might try to raise me. Anyway, don't worry. I'm okay. Just a little car accident, in a blizzard, in a place I don't know. Oh…that sounds….I'm okay. I'm in the Upper Peninsula of Michigan where Ben lives.

There's been a blizzard here. Ridiculous! Four feet of snow at one time. Ben, that's his name, Ben O'Brian…now don't Google him, even though I did… Look, I'll save you the time. He's a retired college English professor, taught at the local college here, Hunter Woods College, and he's a mildly famous poet. Anyway, Dale says Spring blizzards are not unusual here in the Upper Peninsula or U.P. as they call it. He says Spring sometimes doesn't come until June. Oh…oh…Dale is the handyman for everybody here. Nice guy, kind of like cousin Kenny. Real caretaker type. Dips chew you know the kind. This is the handyman, not Ben. Ben is the the professor I'm here to look up, Dale is… Looking at this, I'm seeing it's pretty incoherent. Okay…basics. I'm okay. Had a little car mishap in the U.P. of Michigan. Have warm place to get to in the blizzard. Tell the fam I'm in Fiji. Nothing else. I really like him Bun, Ben that is, but please don't tell the family. I need some time to figure out where this is going. Well, really I need some time just to find him in this snow. He's got family too, as I think I mentioned. Tell you more later. Just don't worry. Love! Be well. Val

   P.S. Remember, Fiji.

Part III: The Flight

So, why didn't I fly into an airport that's a little closer? I tried. There's one in the northern lower peninsula of Michigan which is about 80 miles away, and one in Sault Ste. Marie Ontario that's about 70 miles away, but both of them were socked in by this storm front which is covering the eastern U.P. as they call it, and most of lower Michigan. So, the next available flight got into Sawyer Airfield at midnight. And we were delayed a little by some backups at Minneapolis caused by the storm to the east, and also by a headwind which caused us to have to make three approaches to Minneapolis during which the puddle jumper I took from Iowa bounced around the sky so much that I was the only one who didn't heave.

At one point I looked over and saw the seated, strapped in stewardess saying a rosary. As a travel agent, I have to say, that was bad form for an airline employee. I probably would have been more freaked out, like so many of the other passengers, but as a travel agent, this wasn't my first rodeo and I've never crashed yet. So, anyway, we didn't actually get into Sawyer, near Gwinn, Michigan until about 2 a.m. The rental car was easy. It's a pretty small airport.

Part IV: The Beach

By the time I got to the Michigan 28 turnoff, just south of what must be a fair sized town, because I'd actually heard of it before: Marquette, I was having some serious doubts. This isn't Iowa. I know, buck up travel agent you've been away from home before, but that's not what I mean. I mean, if I'm really going to do, what I'm planning on doing: look Ben up, try to become part of his life. Then this is what I'm going to be part of. This big place, with all these shadowy trees. A little scary in the dark, I have to admit. And what's out in those trees? Animals, yeah, sure, but a spirit too. Something that, haunts this place. It's wild. It's not tamed, like Iowa is. At home, every little field has been trained to do it's trick. What I felt out there, what I felt was that nothing could tame this place.

Nothing could make it…comfy. I thought about Ben. He seemed like a very nice guy. But what wildness, that he must have flowing through his veins just from living here, was in him? Could I deal with it?

About that time I saw a roadside stop, right on the big lake and I thought I'd better just pull off just think it over before I went another mile. So I did. I just pulled off in a roadside stop and I stayed there for about fifteen minutes. I got out, put my coat and my hat on and walked down a little iced over set of stairs down to the beach. Now when you stop off at a rest stop in Iowa, what are you looking for? A bathroom. You don't really expect to stand there next to the biggest freshwater lake in the world. You see it on a map and you think, okay, so if you've see one of the great lakes, you've really seen them all. Great big water disappears at the horizon, but that wasn't it. I stood there and I felt tiny. Just tiny. Here was this big wild lake throwing breakers six feet high up on to the beach. The storm wasn't there yet but it was coming and the wind was starting to swirl, but the sky was still clear. And that's when I looked up. Stars, yeah, but the aurora came out then: the Northern Lights, like big fingers playfully walking across the sky, in and out with just a hint of color and at one point swirling.

This was just so big! This was just so big and so impossible. I was one tiny woman trying to find this man in this big wild country. I felt like a little girl again. I felt like the little girl sitting on Grandpa Traeger's living room floor looking at her atlas, the one Grandpa gave me all those years ago, the one that started all my traveling. Things look so wonderful on a map, and sometimes they are, but this? So, so overwhelming and I just stood there. I couldn't look away. And something, something just said as though it was right next to me, "Be brave."

I thought about Grandpa then, how he'd come back from Japan after World War II, Uncle Herb told me he'd weighed 89 pounds after being in that prison camp. He just came back and went to work on the farm and until he died 15 years ago and we went through his things, nobody would have known, and really we still don't about all the stuff he'd seen. He hadn't even told

Grandma, who, when Bunny asked her about it only said "Leaving well enough alone, darlin' is sometimes the best way through."

Then I remembered something from one of Ben's poems, "To know the stars as friends…" That is his wildness I think. That is his journey maybe: to be part of this, a brother to the stars and the trees and the water and the animals and the spirit of this wild place. That's what I was going to have to try to do too, or at least try to understand in him.

Now which way should I go? Was I up to this? Did I even want it? Should I be brave and just soldier on in the face of all this, well, bigness, or should I just get back in my little car and head back to my little life. Send my farm folks on their trips. Go on a hike or two? Like the John Muir. That took planning, lots of planning. Setting up food everywhere. Walking over mountain passes. Sleeping out in bear country. Making contacts. Making contacts, that was it. Sure, sure I'd been making contacts, building my business, sending people on diversions for years, but this wasn't a damned diversion. This was a life decision. This was, for me at least, as big as this lake, as big as this country, as strange and maybe wonderful as these lights in the sky. My atlas wasn't going to work here.

"Be brave," I said into the night. I didn't know who I was talking to. Maybe just myself. Maybe I was echoing back to Grandpa what he had, without a word, communicated to me. But dammit! I was going to find out.

Part V: Fair and Friendly Warning

I had some breakfast at an overnight diner in a town right on Lake Superior called Munising and despite all my resolve on that beach, now that I was in some place warm, with good comfort food and some coffee in front of me, I thought of the family diner in Harbinger and thought over maybe turning around and going back. I thought about the lights again and that great lake was still staring me in the face. "Leaving well enough alone…" there was Grandma knitting and looking down at me over her glasses while

I looked at an atlas on the floor. Then there was, my ex, William telling me that the business would go belly up without him. And truth was I'd doubled it since he left.

What was the very worst that could happen here? Well, I could get my heart broken and limp on back to Iowa. Then I realized that no matter how dumb it was seeming to keep going into this labyrinth, it would be even dumber to turn around having come this far.

What was the worst that could happen? Well, I could go to all this trouble and get my heart broken and end up limping on back to Iowa. But broken hearts aren't new to me. I've had my own and nursed my daughters and my sisters through them. Being told I can't do something isn't new to me either. So there was no reason to stop here any more than to stop 50 miles west of here. Less, really. I was closer now to whatever was coming. I'd been brave so far. I'd walked over mountain passes, through bear and cougar country. I'd camped out on beaches in southeast Asia. Nothing here was wilder than that. So why was I scared?

"Where ya headed, hon?" said an old fisherman carrying an old olive drab backpack with bits of fishing rod poking out through the straps. He had just sat down at the next table. He looked, with his grizzle of beard and taut leathery face to be in his late 70's. He pulled a mad bomber hat off his head and grinned as he sat down.

"I'm on my way to Hunter, know it?"

"Well, been there a time or two. Over east of Newberry. Well, you'll be there in an hour and a half or so if the blizzard don't kick up that way. It might."

"How…bad can it get?"

"Well, not gonna lie. Pretty bad. But I bet you'll manage."

"Oh, why's that?"

"You look like you manage pretty well, dontcha?"

"Well…" I could't help smiling. "Yes, I do, if I do say so myself. Thanks."

"Y'welcome," He was sipping his coffee which the waitress had brought automatically.

"Going out on the big lake?"

"Got to. That's my job now. I'm retired. Gotta keep my shanty warm and the fish company."

"What do you catch?"

"Whatever bites." He leaned towards me and gave a faux whisper. "Don't tell nobody, but sometimes that ain't much."

"I bet you're a good fisherman."

"How can you tell?"

"Well, you look like you manage pretty well, dontcha?"

He laughed a little laugh of surprise. He finished his coffee in one gulp and stood up to go. He stopped, turned towards me and said, "Watch out on the Stretch."

"The Stretch?"

"Seney Stretch: 26 miles of flat, straight and wild. Lots of deer. Just be careful. Know you will be."

He started for the door, turned back again and said, "Nice to meet you. Don't stare at the snowflakes. They'll drive ya crazy ."
He winked and headed out.

"Thanks. Good luck."

Part VI: The Storm

So, if I wanted to see Ben, and the weather was bad, couldn't I have just waited until the storm cleared? I think, maybe, yeah, but I started thinking about where the legend of the woman on the train must have gotten to in his family's lore by this time and I thought it'd probably reached critical mass, and if I didn't act soon, it might be very weird. Ha, as if it's not now with me standing outside his sister's front door. So, will it be the lady or the tiger, or both? I bet Ben would appreciate my dilemma, and the literary reference… At least, I hope he would.

So, what happened to the car? Well, remember the northern lights I was telling you about? They were just shimmering over the Seney Stretch and since it's 26 miles of straight road, I was just staring at them and thinking about how weird it was that I was here and that maybe it was worth it, even if nothing worked out with Ben just to see this natural display. Just to add one more experience to my traveling experiences, however fleeting the impressions from it might be. What can I say? I'm a travel agent, and what that means is I'm still that little girl who wants to see if what the atlas says is true. So, I kept watching them off and on all the way to the next town after Seney, on M-28: McMillan, then kept on watching them all the way 15 miles past Newberry where I finally saw a sign for Hunter.

All that stuff in Ben's poems is dead on. The trees were alive with the wind, and the sky was alive with the lights. And then the snow stared right back at me. The old fisherman was right. At one point it was the worst blizzard I have ever seen. We get whiteouts in Iowa, but this was just vicious. Oh, and did I mention, there's wolves in the U.P. too. At least one for certain, because I saw him. He wasn't a fox. He wasn't a coyote. I've seen them both and they do not have the size, the high matted ruff, or the, what…the presence a wolf has. This was a wolf on a mission. I saw him in my headlights right at the six miles to Hunter sign, which I had been very grateful to see in whiteout conditions. This wolf just strode up out of the swamp and trotted right in front of me, then right off the other side of the road and slipped in among the shadows of the trees with me just watching him like an idiot, or a little girl looking up from the atlas in her hand. That wolf had some place to go. So did I, but unlike him I had forgotten my purpose. I've been in wild places before and I know enough to know you can't forget your purpose like that in the wild. It doesn't forgive, like tame places. You have to focus. I didn't. And I paid for it. Suddenly I was going off the highway. I exited into the swamp on the west bound side putting a little bump in my bumper and fender and getting hopelessly stuck. When the car came to a stop, and after I tried to back onto the road and failed completely, I sighed, then absently looked off in the direction I'd seen the wolf. I think south. He was long gone, but I'll never forget him. Was I really ready for this?

So, since I was okay…physically anyway…I tried the cell phone, which doesn't work very well here. So I resorted to the Onstar lady from the button in the car. She hooked me up with Triple A who had a bit of a problem believing there was a

Hunter, Michigan, home of the Nimrods by the way. That's the school nickname. I'll have to ask Ben about that one, if I ever see him again. So anyway, at long last, after the complications with Triple A, Onstar, a passing snowplow, (which scared hell out of me), and my silly and pointless battles with my own firm belief I would probably die here, Dale finally arrived in his wrecker. And, a very small town being what it is, in the course of our conversation, between his quick spits of tobacco out the truck window in a blinding snowstorm, Dale told me he was handyman to Ben and the family and many other families in Hunter, and he could take me right to his house. Only trouble was, Ben wasn't home. At this point he grinned at me, and I noticed there were a few stray pieces of tobacco on his not overly brushed teeth, as he said, "Local rumor is that he met a woman on the train west...somebody name of Harlotjer or something"...

"Oh, funny name. And what does he..."

Then his face got a little more serious "...but then I heard a rumor that his dog, Huck...he's got two of 'em, the other one's Tom, (of course I thought smiling to myself) had a pretty bad stroke. And well...Doc loves that dog, so I'm betting he's on his way home or at least to his camp."

"He's camping out in this?" I asked.

This got a big chuckle out of Dale who said, "No...no m'am, around here that's what we call our...uh...cottages, lake houses?"

He looked serious for a moment making sure this outlander understood. When he saw I did, the smile came back again and he said, "You know who would know? His sister Jen. She knows everything about Ben. And she's an early riser, might be up."

The grin hung on extra long. Dale knows the family. He knows, that my showing up at her doorstep might make for interesting times in Hunter. There can't be a lot to do here. Well, at least everybody has a sense of humor even if in this case, it was at my expense.

"Or," he said, then, "I've got Ben's number right here. I could call him for you, or, here..." he held out his slightly antiquated cell phone, "…you could call him yourself."

So, why didn't I take him up on that? Well, the truth is, I'd had Ben's number for a while and been too scared to call him. I'm good on phones, text, email with my customers, but I've never been so hot contacting people I have crushes on by any of those methods. It's always scared me stupid. Of course, when I was in high school, girls didn't call boys. And I married pretty young, and never really got the hang of it all. Besides, I've always figured I have a better shot face to face. Even with my clients, I always like it best when I can look them in the eye in my office. And now that his poor dog was sick, he might not want to see me at all. But I'd come all this way. What if right there in the truck he told me, over the phone, that he didn't want to see me. Being the gentleman he seemed to be, I doubted that would happen, but what if it did? I couldn't risk it. So, I just smiled at Dale and said, "I think I better talk to him face to face."

Part VII: Bunny's Lost Voice Mail

"Come on, Val, pick up. Pick up. Come on! I'm opening up the restaurant here. Pick up. Come on… I don't know whether to call the police, or…Do they even have police…mounties… what… What is all this? Okay, okay. I'll tell the family Fiji, but you're going to explain this all to me, right? Just text or something to show you're okay. Okay. Okay. I gotta go. Love you. And, yeah, count on it. I'm googling this guy first chance I get."

Part VIII: Playing Chicken

So, having made a long story even longer, here I am, standing outside Jen's door in Hunter, Michigan, at 5:57 a.m., in a snowstorm, on the first day of Spring. A second ago I heard a male voice, probably, Jen's husband…Mark…I think. I thought he said, "For once in your life…" So, anyway, they're up for certain. Don't know if that's good or bad.

I can go over right now if I want and wait in the *Hunter*

Fixall Garage nice and warm. Dale would probably give me some coffee and I could be on my way when the storm stopped. But you know what? If I did that, by the time I got to the airport again everybody in Hunter would know I was here. Dale would think I was a coward. I would be letting that old fisherman in Munising down too. More importantly, the little girl with the atlas on Grandma Traeger's floor would never forgive me for being chicken. I suddenly realized a minute ago, that in my life every success I've ever had was almost always the result of my being brave. One thing was for sure: If I didn't try, nothing was going to change. Yes, I could always go home, but if I didn't follow through now, I'd never ever know for sure about any of this and I'd always wonder about what might have been. I've decided that's way worse than a broken heart. Being in doubt would never leave me alone. For 28 years I've been sending farmers off to see the wonders of the world. I've gone along with them a time or two on tours, and seen quite a few wonders myself, including the wonders I've seen tonight. The truth is this: nothing in the world that you only visit, no matter how miraculous, satisfies for more than a few minutes, hours, or days. Then you have to satisfy your heart with memories and pictures. That's just not enough anymore. I'm tired of being a visitor. I need something more. So, whatever the risk, I'm going to be brave. I've been told recently that I manage pretty well. And while old fishermen surely tell some whoppers, they never lie, when it really matters. I believe that.

So Grandpa, I'm going to be brave. Grandma, sorry, but I'm not going to leave well enough alone. Little Val let's put the atlas down and go ring a doorbell.

Here goes.

Chapter 15
New Day

Part I: A New Ben

March 21, 2016: 7:15 a.m.

Ben O'Brian saw his father dressed in camouflage and sitting in a duck blind. He thought he was dreaming, or dead. Then he realized it was only the photograph hanging on the north wall of camp. There was bright light reflecting off the picture.

So I'm alive.

Then another thought quickly occurred to him.

His answer was instantaneous: it was the paw. Ben raised his eyes, and there the big brown dog was, paw outstretched on Ben's arm. Huck's dark brown eyes, under their deeply hooded lids and brows, were focused on Ben. Huck's ears were perked and expectant.

Huck was hungry. Behind the big dog a step or two stood Tom also waiting for breakfast, but, as usual knowing his place in the pecking order.

So, it's a good day!

He got up and felt the stiffness in his back from having slept against the arm chair, went over to the food bins on the front porch and got out the bowls watching Huck the whole time. Not a limp. Not a sag in his right side.

He filled the food bowls wiping away tears. There was a

knock at the door. He looked at the clock, 7:53 a.m.

Ha, Jen, right on time. Nice of her, really. Wait a minute though, when has Jen ever knocked?'

Now he was curious, the dogs, *both his dogs*, engrossed in their food, hadn't heard, or more likely didn't care about the tenuous knock. That could wait for later. It was breakfast time.

Jen, even if she knocked, wouldn't knock like that.

Who's at the door?

The sun was up. The knocking was a little more insistent, and then, that voice.

"Ben?"

Part II: Same Old Jen

March 21: The first day of Spring. The idea that real Spring could come too early in the U.P. ever was always the talk of the sugar shack. This year, though, admittedly after a pretty profound blizzard, March 21 had come up sunny.

Jennifer O'Brian-Hicks had loaned her snowshoes to a woman who had shown up on her doorstep in the wee hours. A woman she only knew second hand or by her probes on the internet until she was standing there, snow-covered and vulnerable in the doorway.

Here she is. Here she is expecting me to go find my brother and ruin his life. Ruin all of our lives. Oh she's a schemer this one. If I let her get her talons into Ben, well... we'll all be the worse for it.

But the woman didn't seem that way. Not at all. She looked...well...nice. And it was also true that she did look somewhat like Grace. Did she owe it to Grace to hear this woman out? Despite her absolute conviction on one level that this woman was going to be a disaster for all concerned, especially Ben, her deeper voice just kept quietly saying, "Hear her out."

"Hello, you must be Jen."

"And you are?" It came out a touch more caustic than she had intended.

"I'm Val Traeger. I'm from Iowa, and I met your brother,

Ben, on the train."

"Yes?"

"Well I wondered if I might…"

Oh Jen, stop it.

"Come in. You must be frozen."

Val flashed a small and incredibly endearing smile, and Jen was hooked.

Dammit, I like her!

A half hour later, after Val had told her story, and Jen had voiced some now feeble attempts at veiled threats which only came out to Val as her deep love and concern for her older brother, Jen loaned Val her snowshoes so she could get down the road to the camp through the deep snow. She drew her a map to the cabin from the end of the road. She even drove her the 20 miles *to* the end of the road. Then, while Val watched, she turned for home.

Two hours later she told Mark she was going back out there. Mark who was about to go out the door to work sighed and said, "I know you're going to anyway, but I wish you wouldn't. You're only going to reinforce everything Ben thinks about you. Ah…maybe that's a good thing. Go ahead."

She had smiled at him over her coffee from the kitchen table as he stood in the doorway, "You know, I don't need your permission."

"I know, but you want it anyway."

"Love you."

"Love you more."

And so she had gotten into her car and again driven the 20 miles to the end of the road where she walked without snowshoes in Val's tracks all the way to the cabin. This was no easy trick since Val's legs were twice as long. She had contemplated taking her skis and simply skiing in, but if she decided not to intrude, then Ben would see the tracks and figure she had anyway. This way, she could get up close, see what she could see, then go back without either of them being the wiser.

Ben's right. I am a little sneak.

But when she'd gotten to the door and heard no dogs bark,

she knew they weren't there.

He's taken her on a walk down to the channel of course. Like that's what she wants to do after traveling across America all night. The big doofus. But, wait. That means Huck's okay! Damn you, Ben, even if he is okay, should you take him on a long walk, he just had a stroke you... That dog. That dog.

She went inside, walked through the living room where the fire was still ablaze on the hearth. Then out to the front porch where the sun was beaming in over the breakfast dishes still on the table.

"They were in a hurry."

She could see two sets of snowshoe tracks and two sets of dog prints along the edge of the lake. She went to the coatrack and took down Ben's binoculars, which were hanging there by a strap. She focused them on the channel and could see them standing there. It looked like Tom was excited as he was bouncing up and down. Huck was standing in one place near the channel, focused on something. Ben and Val were standing close together, really close. They...

"Oh my..."

Quite slowly, reluctantly, she hung the binoculars back on the coatrack. She almost left, but looked at the breakfast dishes on the table.

If I do them he'll know I was here and he'll tease me. Hey, what's this?

There was a note on the table.

"Hey Little Sneak–Huck is fine. I have no idea how that's possible. Went for walk to channel with Val.–Doofus

P.S. Thank you."

Jen scowled, then laughed, hard. Then she stopped and wiped away one tear.

"He *is* right about me. Okay then...so what?"

She picked up the dishes and walked around the open counter to the sink.

"The things I do for this family..."

Epilogue

Up on the peninsula, between the two eastern muddy fingers of Hunter Lake, the wolf stood under towering hemlock trees scenting the air. He could hear the people talking and the young dog barking. He had been headed for the channel for water, but it could wait.

He turned back into the woods and disappeared into the shadows.

Acknowledgements

First thank you to Doc Bradley, F.K.B., Kenny, the old ballplayer and dentist, for making the decision to bring his family north from Midland, Michigan to Hulbert Lake in 1954. At the time he was assured by family that all four of the Bradley children would be eaten by bears. He had faith. When I came along a few years later, however much his faith may have been shaken, he stuck by me until his death in 1973. Speaking of faith, no one had more than Lucy Booth Bradley; teacher, writer, World War II codebreaker, wife and mother to the Bradley brood. How in the world did you two raise us all? And Mom, how did you ever raise me alone? One of life's great mysteries.

And speaking of families, I'd like to thank my on stage family, who appeared with me in *Lake Stories,* the prequel to this novel, on the Lake Superior Theatre stage in 2010: Shelley Russell as Grace, Shannon Miller, my sort of daughter, as Kate, Timmy Grams as Michael, Rob Shirlin as Mark, and the little sneak herself, Monica Nordeen as snoopy ol' Jen. Thanks guys for giving life to these characters. You're not them, but the shadows you played on stage inform the characters here in more ways than you can ever know.

Thank you also to my editing leader Matt Dryer, who selflessly informed me that there was another way beyond making the usual rounds with New York agents, then proceeded to launch me into a world of publication I am only beginning to understand and for which I can never fully repay him. Thank you to my big sister Beth who argued with me over all the nuances until we got it all just right…or right enough. Thanks Beth for looking out for me in life and on the page all these years. And a second thank you to Monica for her tireless and amazing proofreading skills.

Thank you to my big brothers Jim, Tim, and Denny for always being only a phone call away and broad shoulder to cry on. I wouldn't be here at all guys, if you hadn't been. I hope you're pleased with these results. Tim, I'll meet you at the duck blind!

To my nieces and nephews for inspiration, love, and laughs for all these years.

To the faculty and staff of all my working places, *The Marquette Mining Journal, The L'Anse Sentinel, Lansing Magazine, The Newberry News, The Sault Evening News*, Munising High School, Republic-Michigamme High School, Northern Michigan University, and most of all Westwood High School. Thank you everyone for laughs and tears through sometimes pretty trying but ever wonderful years.

To all the dogs through all the years, Mack, Tawny, Brandy, Snowshoe, Sota, Gus, Huck and Tom, for all those great times in the U.P.'s great outdoors.

Finally, to my sons Tag and Pat, the joys of my life. And to my dearest Deb, without whom I could barely take a breath. I love you so.

ABOUT THE AUTHOR

B.G. BRADLEY is a retired high school teacher, former newspaper reporter and columnist, part time college professor, poet, novelist, playwright, director and actor. His fiction, non-fiction, and poetry have appeared in various regional publications including *Detroit Sunday Magazine, Michigan Out-of-Doors, Passages North, Sidewalks, Foxcry Review, The Marquette Mining Journal,* and *The Newberry News.* His plays have appeared on local stages including the Lake Superior Theatre which in 2010 produced his *Lake Stories,* a prequel to this novel, which he wrote, directed, and starred in as Ben O'Brian opposite NMU's Dr. Shelley Russell as Grace. Bradley lives in Diorite with the love of his life, Debbie, and his labrador, Tom. His sons Taggart and Patrick are actors and arts activists on their own.

Coming in 2018:

Summer Rounds

The next installment in the Hunter Lake series by B.G. Bradley!

Battle tested ex-Marine Dale Sylvanus has work to do... not just in the wrecker he drives along the state and county roads around Hunter Lake, in Michigan's rugged Upper Peninsula... and not just as the handyman on the humble homes in the town of Hunter proper, or on the camps and cottages along the shores. Dale's real work is at home where his rock-solid wife, Carrie is patiently waiting for him to get his act together. It's been months since she rightly showed him the door, and Dale knows he's got no one to blame but himself.

His old hometown pals, "The Puppies," have been taking up entirely too much of his time, and as everyone in Hunter knows, though they're mostly harmless, those boys are generally up to no good.

Thankfully, Dale has lots of good friends and family to help him back on the path. There's Father Bill, the free-spirited priest who holds Mass in the little chapel on the lake, and gently finds his way into the lives of the folks around those waters and all around town (whether they're practicing Catholics or not); "Big Ol'" Rex, Dale's boss from the Hunter Fix All Garage; our old friend Jen O'Brian-Hicks, getting the scoop on everyone yet again; Dale's straight shooting, good humored mom and pop; his indomitable youngest son, Donny; his bright, lovely daughter, Kelly, and many others.

Can Dale's friends and family help him find his way back home? And what new surprises lie along the back roads and byways of Dale's home town?

Come back to Hunter Lake in 2018 and join Dale and company as they make their *Summer Rounds*.

Made in the USA
Columbia, SC
03 February 2022